*The Spy Who
Came In from the Sea*

The SPY *Who* CAME IN

Peggy Nolan

Pineapple Press, Inc.
Sarasota, Florida

FROM *the* SEA

Inquiries should be addressed to:

Pineapple Press, Inc.
P.O. Box 3889
Sarasota, Florida 34230

www.pineapplepress.com

Library of Congress Cataloging-in-Publication Data

Nolan, Peggy.
        The spy who came in from the sea / Peggy Nolan.--1st ed.
                p.   cm.
        Summary: A fourteen-year-old moves to Florida at the height of World War II to join his father, a Navy seaman, and soon develops such a reputation for exaggeration that when he announces having seen an enemy spy land on the beach, no one believes him.
                ISBN 1-56164-186-3 (hb.) — ISBN 1-56164-245-2 (pb.)
        [1. Honesty Fiction. 2. Fathers and sons Fiction. 3. Spies Fiction. 4. World War, 1939–1945 Fiction. 5. Florida Fiction.]
        I. Title.
PZ7.N695Sp   1999
[Fic]—dc21

                                        99-32933
                                        CIP

ISBN-13 (hb): 978-1-56164-186-4
ISBN-13 (pb): 978-1-56164-245-8

First Edition
Hb: 15 14 13 12 11 10 9 8 7 6 5
Pb: 13 12 11 10 9 8 7 6 5 4

Illustration on page iii by Steve Weaver
Interior design by *Osprey Design Systems*
Printed in the United States of America

Ages 8–14

For Sean and Sarah

Acknowledgments

I would like to thank Charles Hardison for his tales of real spies, Charlotte Andersen for encouraging me to begin, and Grace Murdock and Diane Sawyer for their invaluable critiques and suggestions. I am indebted to the many librarians who aided me in my research. A special thanks goes to my editor, June Cussen, for her keen eye and guiding hand. To my children and my husband, Richard, who encouraged, supported, and enabled me to write this novel, I am grateful.

Table of Contents

The Spy Who
Came In from the Sea

I

Palm Trees and Alligators

I t's not easy having the name Francis Xavier Leo Aloysius Hollahan. But that was before leaving for Florida. Now I'm Frank. I changed my name on November 22, 1943, when Mom and I boarded the train at Philadelphia's Thirtieth Street Station and headed south.

Sixteen hours later, the engineer sidetracked our train a third time. Four more troop trains barreled past us. One hauled tanks and jeeps, the others carried servicemen in uniform. The war against Germany, Italy, and Japan was going strong, and it seemed like every soldier, sailor, and marine was on the move.

Mom sighed. "Poor Pops. He must be wondering what happened to us."

"He knows how it is," I said. "He'll be waiting."

Mom and I were on our way to join Pops, who had finished naval basic training and been sent to Jacksonville, Florida. Pops' job is patrolling the Eastern seacoast, looking for German U-boats that prowl the Atlantic and attack our ships. But Pops wanted more. He wanted to cross the Atlantic and see some real action. He wrote about going to exotic-sounding places like Casablanca and Algiers.

3

Exotic: from another part of the world, foreign, excitingly differ-
ent. That was one of my eighth-grade spelling words. I liked
the sound of it and I used it every chance I got. But Mom
didn't like the sound of it at all. "What Pops does is exotic
enough for me," she'd said.

At daybreak the next morning, we crossed from Georgia
into Florida. I nudged Mom awake with my elbow. Her
head jerked up. She opened one eye.

"Look, a palm tree!" I said, awed by the sight. The first I'd
ever seen.

"Hmm," Mom said and fell back asleep. Two nights of
sleeping sitting up had taken its toll.

I popped a piece of tutti-frutti in my mouth and
whipped out my old, beat-up, black-and-gray composition
book.

Dear Deidra,

Now there's an exotic name. Deidra was a year ahead of me
in school. She was the best first baseman I ever saw. I never
got up the nerve to say anything more than "hi" to her. But
now that I'm a zillion miles away, I can think of plenty to say.

> *How are you? I am fine. You may not remem-*
> *ber me. I left Jefferson Junior High two days ago*
> *forever, well, at least until the war is over, which*
> *could take some time. Florida is great. Palm trees*
> *all over the place, swaying in the tropical breeze.*

Okay, so I only saw one palm tree and no breeze was
blowing. Some people accuse me of lying, but it's more like
stretching the truth. Funny how you can get a reputation
just by trying to make things a little more interesting.
Anyway, I'm sure I'll be seeing other palm trees, and a

Florida breeze will pick up any minute, and it's bound to be warm and tropical. Hmm, maybe palm trees aren't exotic enough. I'll throw in an alligator. Or two.

> *I saw three alligators sunning themselves beside a pond. They looked mean and ugly. I can't wait to get off the train and see one up close. They don't scare me.*
>
> *Well, got to go. I'll write again when I have an address and you can write me back.*
>
> *Your friend and admirer,*
> *Frank (previously Francis) Hollahan*
>
> *P.S. I think you're a great first baseman.*

Mom woke up and took out her tortoiseshell compact. She flipped it open and dabbed her nose with her powder puff. Sitting next to her, I could see my reflection in the mirror. My blue eyes matched hers, but my dark hair was all Pops. My nose too, which was flat as a pancake. "Cute," Mom said. But what guy wants to be called cute?

Mom glossed her lips with Cherry Red lipstick and smoothed her pageboy hair. She snapped her compact closed. "How do I look?" she asked.

"Spectacular, Mom. Pops will fall down dead when he sees you."

"You really think so?" She grinned.

The steady clackity-clack of the train wheels slowed to a clack. . . clack. . . clack as the train chugged toward the station. A big sign announced JACKSONVILLE. Mom tapped her nails on the armrest. I popped another piece of gum in my mouth and worked it hard. I couldn't wait to see Pops. Three whole months is a long time.

The platform was crowded with sailors, a sea of white broken only by the bright colors of the women's dresses and, as Mom would say, their perky little hats. The blast of the train whistle sent a mother scurrying to grab her little boy's arm and pull him away from the tracks. I leaned against the window. All the sailors looked alike in their bell-bottom trousers and middy tops, but I was sure I would spot Pops.

Mom peered over my shoulder. "Do you see him yet?" she asked.

I was too excited to answer. I pulled on my knuckles until they popped, something I always do when I get edgy. The train jolted to a stop. Steam hissed and bellowed a white cloud from beneath the wheels. Darn, I couldn't see anything.

Lugging our suitcases, I led the way, weaving through the crowds, craning my neck, searching for Pops. Any second now I knew he'd come bursting through the swarm of people shouting, "Francis, my lad." The crowd thinned out pretty fast. Seems like everyone getting off the train had someone to meet him. They gathered their luggage and climbed aboard buses or into cars and cabs.

"St. Augustine. Daytona. Palm Beach. Miami. *Alllll aboard!*" The conductor's voice boomed like he'd bounced it off a mountainside. The people waiting to board scrambled on. Pretty soon Mom and I were the only ones left standing on the platform. The engine started up, and the whistle blew its long, lonely wail as the train disappeared down the track.

Mom smoothed her hair and tried to hide her disappointment, but I heard it in her voice. "Let's wait inside," she said.

I dragged our suitcases in, and we settled on a long

wooden bench. I peeled off my sweater. Florida sure was warm for November. The door to the waiting room swung open, and Mom half rose from her seat. When she saw it wasn't Pops, she sank back onto the bench and gave me a weak smile.

Mom rooted around in her purse and pulled out a dollar bill. "Here, get yourself a hot dog and an orange soda."

"Don't you want one?"

"Francis, I couldn't eat a bite wondering what's happened to your father."

"Don't worry, Mom. He'll be here." But I was getting pretty worried myself. When Pops joined the Navy, he told me I'd have to look after Mom until we joined him again. That was a piece of cake in Philadelphia. But Florida? I sure wish he'd hurry up and get here.

On my way to get the hot dog, I stopped at the glassed-in booth where the station master sat. I cleared my throat. "Excuse me, Mister. Do you have a message for Mrs. Hollahan?"

The station master riffled through a pile of telegrams, shook his head, then checked a bulletin board. "Nope. Nope. Nope," he said as his finger ran down the row of tacked-up notes. "Sorry, son. Nothing here for Hollahan."

We waited two hours. No Pops.

"Well, Francis, there's no doubt our telegram went astray. We'll just have to get ourselves to the naval base and find him."

"Two blocks north," the station master mumbled through a mouthful of chips when we asked directions to the bus. A block away, we spotted a bus marked "Mayport U.S. Naval Air Station." People lined up, waiting to board. According to the schedule, it was the last bus going to Mayport that afternoon.

The driver climbed into his seat and adjusted the mirrors. "Tickets. Tickets, please," he said, punching a hole in each ticket before handing it back.

"Don't let him leave," Mom ordered as she dashed into the bus depot to get our tickets. The last passenger in line climbed aboard. The driver checked his watch and switched on the engine. I placed one foot on the step and kept the other on the curb. I craned my neck looking for Mom. I sent her telepathic messages. *Hurry. Rush. Run.*

The driver shifted gears. "On or off, son. I've got a schedule to meet."

"My Grandma will be here any second."

"On or off," the driver repeated.

I held my ground. I don't know where that grandma came from, but it got me started. "You wouldn't deny an ancient, decrepit old lady a last glimpse of her grandson before he ships out, would you? He might be killed and never come home except in a coffin." I gave him my basset-hound look, all sad and droopy.

He wasn't buying it. The driver rolled his eyes and gripped the handle that closed the door. Let him crush me like a melon—I wasn't moving.

But where was Mom?

I kept talking. "Grandma's got rheumatism. Bad! If you left, she'd faint dead away. I know you wouldn't want that on your conscience."

"Son, back off that step. Now."

I was running out of ideas when I heard Mom's voice. "Here I come," she called, waving the tickets and tripping along on her four-inch heels.

"That's your grandma?" asked the driver.

I smiled.

"Get on," he said, jerking his thumb. He was still shaking

his head halfway to the base. Yep, sometimes my story-telling comes in handy.

The bus dropped us off outside the Mayport Naval Air Station's main gate. A cluster of low, white buildings blistered by the Florida sun stood beyond. A dozen more were going up nearby. Bulldozers worked to clear more land. In an inlet, I could see the yachts and fishing boats that the government had taken over from civilians to use as patrol boats for the duration of the war. I wondered which one Pops operated. Maybe he was out on patrol and that's why he couldn't meet us.

The guard at the main gate waved in jeeps, lorries, lumber trucks, a cement truck, a derrick, and dozens of military vehicles, one after another. Each military vehicle received a smart salute from the guard as it rumbled past. Three sailors walked in ahead of us, each flashing an identification card.

"Come on, Francis," Mom said and started past the guard.

"Whoa, there, little lady. You can't come in here."

"But we've come all the way from Philadelphia," Mom said, as though that were reason enough to let us in.

"Sorry, ma'am," he said.

Mom put on her best smile. "It seems there's been a mix-up. Our train arrived twelve hours late, and my husband wasn't able to meet us. He's stationed here and patrols for U-boats. He must be on duty." Mom straightened her shoulders and stood a little taller. She sure was proud of Pops. "Do you know where we can find him?"

"I couldn't let you in if I did know. No pass, no entry. Tell me his name and rank and I'll see what I can find out." I watched him on the phone through the open door of the guardhouse. He was back a minute later. "You did say

Seaman Ted Hollahan, didn't you, ma'am?"

Mom nodded.

"Sorry, but he completed gunnery training two days ago. He shipped out on a carrier."

"But that's impossible," Mom argued.

"Ma'am, with the Navy, anything is possible."

2

New Territory

My mouth dropped open. Pops gone! Mom clutched her purse. Her knuckles turned white. I watched her eyes go from wide to narrow, then wide again. Finally, she took a deep breath and collected herself.

"There's nothing to do, Francis, but rent ourselves an apartment and wait to hear from Pops." She nodded her head emphatically, and I knew not to argue.

Mom agreed with me, though, that we needed something to keep up our strength. We found an ice-cream parlor and ordered chocolate sundaes. Mom bought a newspaper. She spread it out on the table and ran her finger down the "Apartments for Rent" column, which was very short. "Ouch! Forty-six dollars for an apartment. We can't afford that." I heard a few more ouches, then, "Here's one. 'Sunny, two-bedroom apartment, furnished, one block off beach.'" She stopped and her smile disappeared. "'Military families need not inquire.'" Mom's eyes flashed.

"Who wants their crummy old apartment anyway?" I said, trying to cheer her up.

Mom punched my arm. "That's telling 'em, Francis," and she put her nose back in the paper. "Too far. Too much. Unfurnished." Mom looked up. "It's back to Philadelphia for us," she said.

Pops told me to take care of Mom, and I wasn't about to call it quits. "What about this column, 'Houses for Rent'?"

"We couldn't possibly afford a house, Francis."

I pointed and read. "Frame house, near beach, furnished. Twenty-six dollars a month. South of Jacksonville Beach on Ponte Vedra Road."

We grabbed a taxi and rode south past houses, beach cottages, and hotels. "Golly, there are sailors everywhere," Mom exclaimed.

"Yep," said the driver. "The government took over the hotels and filled 'em full of sailors, most of 'em here for training."

We passed through a couple of small beach towns. Pretty soon there was nothing much to see but sand dunes covered with stubby palms. Every now and then, we caught a glimpse of the ocean. We turned off the highway. The scrub palms gave way to tangled thickets of small trees bent by the wind. "Bayberry," said the taxi driver. Seconds later, we pulled into a grove of huge oak trees with gray lacy stuff hanging from the branches. "Spanish moss," offered the driver.

The taxi stopped in front of a tiny frame house with a tin roof. The landlord, in a big house across the road, came to meet us. Before he could open his mouth, Mom said, "We'll take it." And she hadn't even set foot inside.

Other than the landlord's place and our postage-stamp house, there wasn't another house in sight. The whole area seemed pretty desolate. Inside, the house looked even smaller. One long room served as living room, dining room, and kitchen. I could hardly turn around in the bathroom. The two cubbyhole-size bedrooms ran across the back and faced east. There were no closets. Maybe the house didn't look like much, but the ocean was close, just past the trees and over the sand dunes. I planned to spend a lot of time on the beach.

Saturday I wrote Deidra another letter to let her know my new address. I told her about our house and the beach. I got a little carried away and used words like *fantastic, incredible, magnificent.* I told her I went to a terrific school too, even though I wouldn't even see the building until after the weekend.

Monday I missed the bus and had to walk the two miles to Beach Junior High. I told Mr. Moore, the principal, all those things he needed to know, like my name, address, and where I went to school last. He rose from his desk, unfolding like an accordion. My eyes followed him up and up. I waited for his head to hit the ceiling. It didn't, but his height was astounding. Handing me a note, he said, "Take this to Mr. Jolly in Room 305. Down the hall to the right, fifth door on your left." Mr. Moore gave me a pat on the back and a push out his office all at the same time. I did a quick hop-slide past his gargantuan shoes.

Classes had already begun, so I took my time and scrutinized each classroom I passed. A fresh start. New territory to conquer. I'd take 'em by storm. I reached Room 305, threw open the door, and stepped inside. Every head in the room turned. A hundred pairs of eyes riveted on me.

"Step right in," boomed Mr. Jolly. "Right this way to the Class of the Magnificent Twenty-Seven." Mr. Jolly swept his arm across his chest and gave a deep bow.

Weird! I looked over my shoulder to see if he was talking to someone behind me.

"Aha, a note," he said, snatching the paper from my hand. "Laaaadies and gentlemen and alllll my distinguished students, I introduce to you our new pupil, Frank Holla-han. Today, we become the Magnificent Twenty-Eight. A

good round number, divisible by two and fourteen and . . .
what other numbers, Frank?"

"One and twenty-eight," I shot back.

Mr. Jolly leaned forward. "Continue."

"Uh, four." I scratched my chin.

"And?" Mr. Jolly's flabby jowls jiggled as he nodded his
head in encouragement.

Who was this man with three strands of hair plastered
over his bald scalp? He couldn't really be a teacher, could
he? But there he was, standing in front of the class and
making me perform like a monkey. I scratched my head and
under my arm. I couldn't help myself. Some girls giggled,
and I heard a few snorts from the guys.

"Let's see." I cracked my thumb knuckle. Now I really did
have to stop and think. "Seven goes into twenty-eight. Yeah,
definitely seven."

"Excellent. I believe we have a scholar in our midst."
There were a few more snorts from the back of the room.
"Will Frank be a mathematician, a juggler and tamer of
numbers?" Mr. Jolly continued. "Ah, only time will tell."

He glanced down at the paper I'd handed him. "I see that
you are from Philadelphia, the City of Brotherly Love. Tell
us about yourself."

Why do teachers like to put new kids on the spot? I wish
they'd make everyone in the class stand up and tell something about himself or herself instead. That would sure
help a new kid know who he wanted to hang out with. I
pulled at my knuckles. It helped get my mind working.
"Let's see, uh . . . I like sports, especially football. Not to brag
or anything, but I'm a natural-born athlete."

I heard a snicker from the back of the room. Mr. Jolly
cleared his throat and glared down the third aisle.

I stuck my thumbs in my belt and squared my shoulders,

like Pops does when he's about to set me straight. "Some people think just because I'm short and on the lean side, I'm not good at sports. The truth is, I'm what you'd call sinewy. And I'm tough." I glared down the third aisle. "I might not look like a football player, but I can pass like a pro. I've got terrific coordination."

A girl with golden-brown eyes leaned on her desk and rested her chin in her hand. She was drinking in every word I said. She looked a lot like the Deidra I'd left behind. But, oh, those butterscotch eyes! I directed my words toward her. The rest of the class kind of faded away, which was not a good thing. I started bragging.

"I like basketball too," I said. "Last year I scored more points than anyone else on my team." I didn't bother to mention that the team's average score in a game was nineteen. The girl with butterscotch eyes bent forward. She looked impressed. I tried to stop, but my mouth kept going. "My batting average in baseball is five hundred, and I have a terrific pitching arm. I swim fifty yards under water without taking a breath. I can drive a golf ball two hundred yards." I stopped. I would probably drown before reaching the five-yard mark, and I'd never hit a golf ball in my life.

I took a breath. A deep breath. And I got control of myself. I tore my gaze away from the girl with the golden eyes and turned to Mr. Jolly. "Well, uh, you get the picture."

"Very interesting, Frank," Mr. Jolly said. "We look forward to seeing those talents in the future." I wasn't sure, but I thought I detected a note of sarcasm in his voice.

"Howard," Mr. Jolly said, pointing a fat finger at a tall boy with red hair and freckles, "it will be your duty to show Frank the ropes." Howard's lower lip popped out and his thumb went up. I guessed that meant okay. He never cracked a smile.

"One seat left under the big top, Mr. Hollahan. Settle in."

I took the only empty seat, third from the back beneath a window and right behind Howard.

Mr. Jolly raised one eyebrow and grinned. He shuffled his feet in a little dance. I blinked. "Mr. Jolly sure acts strange," I whispered.

Howard covered his mouth with the back of his hand. "Summers he works for the circus. Stood in for the ringmaster once. Never forgot it."

"As I announced earlier," Mr. Jolly said, "we will begin the day with a spelling bee."

I rubbed my hands together. "Right up my alley, Mr. Jolly. Hollahan's my name. Spelling's my game."

I leaned toward Howard. "I'm a sure winner."

Howard turned and gave me a strange look, like my brains were sticking out and they weren't a pretty sight. But what did I care? My first day, and I'd have a chance to outspell them all. And that was no lie. Let Mr. Jolly ask me to spell *exotic, rendezvous, grotesque, bodacious.* I was ready.

We lined up on either side of the room. Girls against boys. Across from us, I could see the girls smiling nervously and looking down at their feet. No confidence whatsoever. All but a girl named Gladys, who eyed us with disdain. *Disdain: to regard or treat with haughty contempt, d-i-s-d-a-i-n.*

I leaned forward and glanced down my row. The boys looked like a bunch of peacocks. Howard jutted out his chin and waved his thumbs in the air. The boy next to him, Joey, I think, was bouncing around on his toes, jabbing the air and the guys on either side of him. Obviously, he was used to winning. They might be good spellers, but I could lick them all.

Easy words flew from Mr. Jolly's mouth, and everyone made it through the first round. In the second, the girls fell like flies, but three boys went down too. Then it was my turn. I was ready. I'd tackle *leprechaun, lichen, linoleum*. Come on, Mr. Jolly. I can field anything you have to give.

"Frank," Mr. Jolly said. "Principal. Mr. Moore is the principal of our school. Principal."

Oh, so he planned to go easy on me because I'm new. Okay, but I'd show him. I'd still be around when he called those hard and torturous words like . . .

Mr. Jolly's voice cut into my thoughts. "Do I need to repeat your spelling word, Frank?"

"No, sir, Mr. Jolly." I threw my chest out. "Principle. P-R-I-N-C-I-P-L-E. Principle."

Gladys giggled. The second I heard her, I realized what I'd done. I slapped my forehead. What a jerk! "Sorry, Frank," Mr. Jolly said. He looked really sad. "You may take your seat." I opened my mouth to ask for another chance but thought better of it. I sat.

"Great going," mumbled Howard, who'd been the first to go down. "Some champion speller you turned out to be. Don't you know *principal* from *principle*? I'll bet you play football like you spell."

Howard was stuck with me for lunch period. I sat at the table with him and his friends, Joey, the sparring boxer who looked tough, and Lloyd, who was stocky and on the quiet side. They pretty much ignored me. After a while Joey's curiosity got the best of him. "Where do you live?"

"Kind of out in the middle of nowhere about two miles south of town in a swell house right off the beach." Swell might be a slight exaggeration, but it was near the beach. "And there's a lake across the road right behind a big house where our landlord lives."

Lloyd leaned past Joey. "That sounds like old man Kinchloe's place."

"Yeah, that's his name."

Howard threw his head back and laughed. "Swell house? That's nothing but an old chicken coop you're living in. Old Man Kinchloe slapped plywood on the frame of a broken-down coop and put in a couple windows. Why do you think the bathroom sticks out on one side like a rooster's tail?"

Howard roared until he choked. "Bet you pay a fortune in rent. That skinflint Kinchloe doesn't care anything about the war effort. He plans to get rich off suckers like your family."

That did it. I wanted to punch Howard in the nose, but he was up and on his way before I could get out of my seat. I popped a couple of pieces of gum in my mouth, went outside, and leaned against the wall, watching the action. The girls kind of drifted from one place to another, led by gawky Gladys Flagg. When she stopped, they clumped up around her like pins to a magnet. They whispered, glanced at the guys tossing a football, then at me and whispered some more. I felt red creeping up my neck. I turned away and watched the guys with the football.

"Hey, Hollahan, catch," Howard yelled as he spiraled the ball in my direction. I jumped away from the wall, reached up, and pulled the ball down into my chest. Pretty spectacular, if I say so myself. I launched the football for a quick return.

"Not bad, Hollahan. Come on over." I trotted over to the guys, glad for the challenge. We tossed the ball around. I showed them my stuff, and they liked what they saw.

"Our guys challenged Midford Junior High to an after-school game on Wednesday. We could use a good passer, but you don't look like much of a runner. How's your speed?"

"Hey, I practically dance to the goal line. They don't call me Fleetfoot Francis, uh, I mean Frank, for nothing." Actually, no one ever called me that, but I wasn't about to let a little thing like speed get in my way. I'd show them I had what it takes.

Howard's lip popped out and his thumb went up. "Okay. You're in."

Now all I had to do was prove myself.

3

Walking on Jell-O

When I got home, I took a good look at our house. It really was a chicken coop! I even noticed feathers trampled in the dirt by the front door.

Mom was curled up in a chair, doing her nails and listening to *The Guiding Light,* her favorite soap opera. I got myself a hot dog from the icebox, took a couple of bites, and waited. Finally the smooth voice on the radio announced, "Ivory soap. Gentle enough for a baby's skin."

Mom sat up. She rejoined the world. "How did you like your new school? Do you have any homework? Did you make friends?"

"Okay, I guess. No. Kind of." I took another bite.

"Francis, what have I told you about eating raw hot dogs?" She didn't wait for an answer. "And what do you mean 'just okay'?"

"Aw, I messed up in a dumb spelling bee. The guys think I'm a jerk, a mouth with no brains."

Mom waved her hands in the air, drying her Cherry Red nails. "Give it time," she said.

"Well, I did toss around a football with some of the guys. They're playing against another school Wednesday afternoon. They asked me to join them."

"See?" Mom said.

I didn't want to bother Mom with my running problem, so I just nodded and stuffed the rest of the hot dog in my mouth. "I'm going down the beach and look around. Okay?"

Mom tossed aside a nail file, switched off the radio, and popped out of her chair. "Mind if I tag along? I've got some news."

I spun around. "You heard from Pops?"

"Not that good," she said. We let the screen door slam behind us and headed for the beach. "But, my news is prrrretty big." She paused like an actress ready to deliver her best line. "I got a job."

My mouth dropped open. "No kidding?" Mom never worked a day in her life. She had always stayed home and taken care of Pops and me.

"Francis, how could I sit home knowing that Pops is out there somewhere risking his life for us and our country? No more just tearing up old sheets for bandages or knitting warm socks for the GIs. That's important," she said, "but now I'm fit and free enough to do more. I'll be giving my all for the war effort."

"Doing what?" I asked.

"It's all so exciting, Francis. They need riveters at the shipyard. I'll go into an on-the-job training program. If I can sew a dress seam, I can learn to put a metal seam together with a rivet gun. Francis, this shipyard delivers a liberty ship every twenty-seven days. Can you imagine a four-hundred-and-forty-one-foot-long ship completely built in less than a month?"

Mom was still talking when we climbed the last sand dune and stepped onto the windy beach. The fresh salt breeze whipped our hair as we crunched through the sand. Suddenly, Mom stopped. She held her hand out in front of her and studied her perfectly manicured nails. "Golly, you don't think being a riveter will ruin my nails, do you?"

"Not if you have anything to say about it."

Mom laughed and threw her arm across my shoulders. "Isn't this a great place to wait for Pops? I sure do miss him. Where do you suppose he is now?"

"Out there, somewhere," I said, facing the vast expanse of the gray-green ocean.

Mom gave me a hug. "Don't you worry, Francis. Pops will be all right. I know it in my heart." Then she turned away really quick. Her voice got high and chirpy, like when she pretends everything is okay.

"I'd better go start dinner. Would you like calf's brain, cow's tongue, or pig's feet?"

My stomach flipped, and I must have turned green. Mom giggled. "Only kidding," she said. "Francis, you are one lucky boy. A delivery of ground beef arrived at Koon's Cash Store right before I did. And I had enough ration coupons for a whole pound."

Boy, was that good news. I knew the day might come when I found brains on my plate. We got a lot of odd stuff because most of the good meat went to our servicemen. Mom must have read my mind. She said, "Just think, Pops might be wolfing down a juicy steak right now."

Mom turned to leave, and I started off down the beach. "Watch for Pops' ship," Mom called after me, even though we both knew he wouldn't be coming home for a long time, maybe a very long time. Maybe not at all. But I didn't want to think about that. I picked up a broken shell and sent it sailing out into the Atlantic.

I walked north along the beach that stretched before me like a smooth white runway as far as I could see. Not another soul anywhere. Not even a footprint to show anyone had ever been here. Every now and then a path cut through the dunes, leading back to the main road that paralleled the coastline. In the distance I saw a building set into the dunes. As I drew close I came first to steps leading up to a wooden deck built at the top of a sand dune. On the far side was a parking lot. On the beach side sat a long, narrow building with great, wide double doors, facing the ocean. Each padlocked door was a different color. The place was deserted.

What a strange building. I couldn't figure out what it was for. A sign read CABANAS. Never heard of them. Were they first cousins to bananas? I rolled the letters around on my tongue and made a note in my head to check the dictionary. I had never met a word I didn't want to know. The wind gusted and rattled the padlocked doors. A steady bang, bang, bang somewhere deep inside gave me the creeps. Time to go.

I hurried back along the beach in the growing dusk. Before I turned up our path, I took one last look at the ocean. No Pops, just a string of small boats patrolling for the German U-boats. Darn those lurking submarines, gliding silently beneath the surface waiting to blow up our ships. I balled up my fists. They'd better not hurt Pops.

I turned away and jogged home.

◀ ◀ ◀

The next day, school felt like walking on Jell-O, sometimes smooth and sometimes shaky. It started out pretty smooth. We diagrammed sentences and worked on simple algebra problems. I breezed through them both.

Then things turned shaky. Howard cornered me at the

water fountain. "Football practice after lunch. Be there. First, we'll race, just you and me." He turned to Joey. Out came the lip and up went the thumb. "We'll see just how fast old Fleetfoot Frank is."

Doggone Howard. There would be no thumb-up if he saw me run. He'd kick me off the team before I had a chance to play. But I knew once they realized the value of my passing arm, my speed wouldn't matter. I rubbed my biceps and circled my arm, dreading noon rolling around. Just before the bell rang, Mr. Jolly made an announcement. The Jell-O stopped shaking.

Mr. Jolly smoothed down his three strands of hair, then swept his arm up in a Statue of Liberty pose and cleared his throat. "Laaaadies and gentlemen and allll the Magnificent Twenty-Eight, we have been given a mission, an honor, a fortuitous adventure. As you are all aware, Jacksonville and the beach towns are sponsoring a gigantic bond rally on Saturday, the eleventh of December, at the St. Johns River Shipyard.

"Because of my experience in the circus as ringmaster, I have been asked to preside as master of ceremonies at the rally. Naturally, I consider you, my Magnificent Twenty-Eight, to be an important part of this venture. We will plan it together. Perhaps some singing, dancing, acrobatics? We will sell enough war bonds and raise enough money for the government to build a dozen liberty ships."

The girls squealed and clapped. Their faces beamed. I could see Gladys already appointing those who would help her in whatever task Mr. Jolly assigned her. Butterscotch eyes, whose name I'd discovered was Rosemarie, listened to the other girls' jabbering. We guys, on the other hand, slouched down in our seats, leery of the whole business.

"Ladies, ladies, quiet please. Gentlemen, look alert. We

will begin our preparations today by establishing an A-one marching unit. We will perform with the precision of a military drill team. You will make our city proud. You will bring great honor to Beach Junior High and to Jolly's Magnificent Twenty-Eight. Report to me on the blacktop the moment you have finished lunch."

Moans came from Howard. He could no longer have his race with me or his practice. I tried to act just as dejected. Secretly, I screamed, "Hallelujah!"

"After school, Hollahan," Howard said.

"Sorry, not today. My mom's got errands for me, and she's a holy terror if I'm late."

"Yeah, sure," Howard said, sarcasm oozing from his mouth like green slime.

I shrugged. "Hey, I'm the man of the house. She depends on me."

And boy did she ever. She had me putting up curtain rods, scrubbing down walls, moving furniture from one corner to another. Between chores and homework, I didn't have the time or the energy to worry about the football match. But the next morning when Mom said, "Good luck in the game," my stomach muscles bunched into a zillion knots.

4

Game Time

Our Beach Eleven, named the Beach Sharks by Joey, arrived at the mutual territory, a vacant lot halfway between our schools. We tossed the ball around, waiting for the other team. "Here they come," shouted Joey. He rolled up on the balls of his feet as a dozen guys with shoulders as broad as battleships swaggered down the middle of the street. Their shortest player made two of me. My mouth went dry.

"You sure these guys are only in junior high?" I asked. "They look like they've been shaving for years."

Even Howard looked surprised. "I've never seen half these guys before."

"We were short," said a big moose. "We had to pick up a few extras along the way."

"Gee, I don't know," Howard said. The rest of us stared, our mouths gaping.

"What's the matter? You going to chicken out on us?"

With our honor at stake, Howard's bottom lip shot out and his thumb went up.

"Ha! Not a chance. Like always, we play till the street lights come on." The rest of us closed our mouths, stepped closer, and tried to look tough.

That's when Mr. Jolly pulled up to the curb in an old beat-up 1938 Ford station wagon. Gladys, Rosemarie, and a ton of other girls tumbled out like clowns from a circus car. Geez, I didn't know we were going to have spectators.

"We're here to cheer for you," Gladys called. "Ready, Rosemarie, Betty, Janet?"

The four girls stepped forward and faced the others. They yelled, "Two, four, six, eight," punching the air with a fist for each count. "Who do we appreciate? Beach! Beach! Gooooo Beach!" They ended their cheer with one knee on the ground and an arm extended.

I thought they looked swell, but Howard knew a distraction when he saw one. "If you're going to cheer, do it between plays, not when we're in the middle of one," he yelled. Then, turning to us, he growled, "Let's get this game rolling. Flip the coin."

The Midford team won the toss and decided they wanted the ball kicked to them. Joey kicked the ball twenty yards, and the moose returned it forty. Two more plays and they scored. Every time we ran the ball, we hit a solid wall of muscle. By the time we took a break, my battered muscles whimpered with pain.

"Why aren't we passing?" I asked. I figured it was our only chance, and I could show them how to do it if Howard would only give me the chance.

Most of the guys had a dazed look in their eyes. But a few managed to nod their agreement.

"Okay, know-it-all Hollahan," Howard said, making the call as usual, "you get the star position. You guys on the line, hold the monsters back long enough for Yankee-Doodle here to get off a pass. Joey, you'll be on the receiving end."

Lloyd, playing center, snapped the ball to me. I stepped back to make the catch.

"Knock 'em, rock 'em. Give 'em heck," screamed Gladys. I just about jumped out of my skin. The ball bounced off my chest.

Howard yelled at the cheerleaders, then at me. "Catch the ball, big mouth."

The next play the girls kept quiet. I caught the ball and faded back to pass. Wham! I got decked and went down hard. By then I'd figured out why Howard had given me the glory spot. Once more I fell back for a pass, and once more I was flattened by the steamrolling Midfords. Midford continued to score with the ease of pros. By the time they'd racked up thirty-nine points to our big fat zero, my body felt as limp as overcooked noodles.

The sun dropped behind a low cloud bank, and I figured the game would soon be over. I couldn't give up now. I had told the guys I was tough. I'd show them I could take it.

After Midford scored for the seventh time, we got the ball. Our team finally found their weak spot and started blocking their line. I got off a terrific pass. Midford didn't see a need to cover our man downfield. They left Joey wide open to receive my pass. He caught the ball and charged like crazy for the goal line.

We scored!

We slapped each other on the back, hooted, and flashed the "V for victory" sign. The girls screamed, "Frank, Frank, he's our man! If he can't do it, nobody can!" Mr. Jolly whipped his red handkerchief around in a circle above his head and cheered.

Now Midford had the ball. They scored again, but we'd tasted success and wanted more. I planned to dazzle them with another great pass. We huddled. Howard jutted out his lower lip and upped his thumb. "I'll take it from here, Hollahan. Get downfield and be ready to catch my pass."

Howard yanked the glory right out of my hands. He asked me to take the football in. Good grief! If I caught the ball, I'd have to run.

We lined up in T formation. I loped downfield, hoping I'd get in place before Howard threw the pass. Looking back, I saw the ball spiraling towards me. I reached up, felt the leather solid in my hand. Spinning around, I tucked that ball into my chest and kept running. Not a man around me. I'd reach that goal line before they could catch me. I could do it. I plowed forward down the field, my feet like two lead anchors, even heavier than the way they usually felt when I ran.

"Pick up your feet!" Howard screamed.

"Go, Frank, go!" yelled our cheering section.

I pumped my knees. I passed midfield, ten more yards, fifteen. I could hear the guys thundering down the field behind me, practically feeling their breath hot on my neck. I was running for the goal.

Wham! My knees buckled with the hit. I pitched forward, tasted grass and mud . . . way short of the goal. The whole Midford team piled on top of me.

"Street lights," shouted Joey, our signal to end the game. The Midford players scattered like buzzards after a big feed. I staggered to my feet and hobbled over to the other guys. Boy, I was so whipped I felt like mashed potatoes.

"Geez, Hollahan, you run like a lazy loping dog on a hot summer day."

I didn't appreciate the comparison, but I admired Howard's way with words. Not as good as me, but not bad.

"Maybe running's not the best part of my game," I said, "but my pass gave us our only score. Give me a little credit, will you? I saved us from total disaster."

"I'll call it fifty-fifty," Howard said. "About half that stuff you tell us is believable. Guess that makes you only half bad. Ha-ha!"

"Much better than that," Rosemarie said, as she hopped into Mr. Jolly's car.

I hobbled home. It was a long, lonely walk in the dark. My elbows were scraped raw, my muscles whimpered, and my feet definitely dragged. If it weren't for thoughts of Rosemarie's last words, I never would have made it.

5

In from the Sea

When I finally dragged my bruised and battered body within sight of the house, I noticed there wasn't a crack of light shining from the windows. As I fumbled with the doorknob, something square and white, flapping against the screen, caught my eye. A safety pin held it in place. I unpinned the paper, pushed through the door, and closed it behind me. Before turning on a light, I closed the blackout curtains. Mom hated them, but our landlord said better to be safe from enemy ships than sorry. "What they can't see they can't fire on," he said.

The paper had my name sprawled across it in handwriting I didn't recognize. I unfolded the paper, hoping it would explain where Mom was.

Frank,

> *Your mother called and asked me to leave you this note. She has to work double shift tonight and won't be home until the last bus about midnight.*

Your landlord,
Mr. Kinchloe

Oh, boy. What a disappointment.

I showered in the rooster tail. The hot water sure felt good coursing over my aching muscles. But the iodine I dabbed on my elbows nearly sent me screaming into the night. I found a couple of raw hot dogs and potato salad in the icebox and wolfed them down. For dessert I had tutti-frutti gum. I started to toss the wrapper but figured it was time to start saving the foil again. There wasn't much we didn't save. Paper, rubber bands, any old bits of metal, bacon grease (when we were lucky enough to get bacon). The government said they needed this stuff for the war. I wondered what they did with it all. Whatever it was must be good because we had beaten Italy and were pushing back the Germans and Japanese.

I flicked on the radio and turned the dial to *I Love a Mystery*, my favorite. Pops' too. When that was over, I hauled out my homework and ground my way through a long explanation about gravity and a guy named Sir Isaac Newton.

Nine o'clock. What to do? In my bedroom, which was the size of the janitor's closet at school, I pulled out my *Know Your Enemy* charts and thumbtacked them to the wall. Those silhouettes of enemy ships and planes were just what my room needed. I covered the names of the ships with the palm of my hand and identified every last one of them just by looking at the outlines. "Not bad, Hollahan," I congratulated myself. "Not bad at all." By nine-thirty, I'd run out of things to do, so I stuck another piece of gum in my mouth, grabbed my jacket, and headed for the beach.

Boy, was it dark. No moon, but there must have been a zillion stars in the sky to keep me company. The sound of the waves breaking on the beach let me know I'd come to the last dune. Then the wind blowing in from the sea hit me full in the face. *Brrr!* I pulled my collar up around my neck and crammed my hands into my pockets.

Settling down in the tall sea grasses, I lay back and stared up at the stars. The sand beneath, still warm from the sun, felt great on my back. Right off, I spotted Mars, high in the eastern sky, by its reddish color. Clouds drifted across Mars and moved on. I looked north and found the Little Dipper with the North Star at the tip of its handle. Pops had taught me all about the stars and how they had guided ships at sea for thousands of years. Now they had a new thing called "radar" that made it easier. But if that failed, Pops said, they could still follow the stars.

I got to thinking. Wouldn't it be something if Pops happened to be looking up at these very same stars right at this exact same minute? Wouldn't that be swell?

There I was, lying on the beach, minding my own business, and thinking about Pops, when *Thunka! Thunka! Thunka!* The ground began to throb like a giant heart.

Thunka! Thunka! Thunka!

Holy cow! What was going on?

I eased up on my elbow, the earth still vibrating under me, and peered into the darkness. Just beyond the breakers, something huge hovered on the horizon. I smelled oil, the same smell as when lumber trucks rumbled past me on their way to the paper mill. Diesel fuel.

Thunka! Thunka! Thunka!

I strained my eyes, knowing it had to be a ship. It was as long as a football field. Flat on top except for some kind of tower and a huge mounted gun.

Thunka! Thunka! Thunka!

Good gravy, it was a submarine! Exactly like the German U-boat on my *Know Your Enemy* ship chart. It was stuck on the sandbar not thirty yards away. Goosebumps as big as apples popped out on my arms.

The throb of the diesel engines changed to the whine of an electric engine. The sub had freed itself from the sandbar and was heading for the open waters. In seconds, it disappeared in the darkness. I rubbed my eyes and wondered if I'd really seen what I thought I had seen. But when the wind blew the stale stench of diesel oil right up my nose, I knew I hadn't dreamed it.

Before I could scramble up, something moved off to my left, down at the water's edge. I stared. I couldn't believe my eyes. A man scrambled out of a raft and staggered through the surf carrying a good-size chest on his shoulder. The raft disappeared into the ocean as if it were pulled by a rope.

The hair stood up on the back of my neck, and, cold as it was, I felt sweat trickle down my face. I slipped behind a clump of palmettos and flattened myself against the sand. The man hauled the chest up to the dunes, not far from where I was hiding. I swear I could hear his heavy breathing above the sound of the surf and wind. Could he hear my heart pounding? I kept low.

In no time, he dug a big enough hole to bury the chest, and he slid the chest into it. Just as quickly, he covered it over with sand. The man turned north and hurried along the beach. I thought I saw him cut into the dunes and head for the main road. The pounding of the surf grew louder and the wind picked up. Clouds raced across the sky.

Boy, did I ever want to know what was in that chest! But I wasn't about to chance getting caught. I waited a few minutes to make sure he was gone, then I hightailed it home. What a story to tell the guys! I could hardly believe it myself. A German U-boat and a spy coming right out of the sea! I wouldn't have to stretch the truth this time. The news would knock their socks right off 'em.

Raindrops splattered the ground as I ran back to the house.

6

Getting Out the Word

I awoke with a start. The rain beat down on the roof, and thunder rumbled in the distance. I bolted off the couch where I'd fallen asleep trying to wait up for Mom. The clock read eight thirty-five. Oh boy, was I ever going to be late for school. A note was propped on the table beside me.

I missed the last bus and didn't get home until 6:30 this morning. We need a car. DON'T WAKE ME.

Mom

That settled it; she'd just have to wait to hear my news. I pulled on my clothes, grabbed a banana, and bolted out the door.

I burst into the classroom, eager to tell my spy story, but class had already started. Another spelling bee. I went down on the first round with a hoot from Howard. Who could think about spelling at a time like this? I struggled with the class through sentence diagrams, the Revolutionary War, and some word problems involving fractions and percentages. Finally, the lunch bell rang.

I fell into step beside Howard. "Boy, have I got news. After the game yesterday, I went home and walked down to the beach. You won't believe what I saw."

"Probably not," Howard said. Joey and Lloyd laughed.

"It was dark, but I saw the outline clear as day. A U-boat. Stuck on a sandbar." I paused, letting my news sink into Howard's thick brain.

Howard turned his thumbs down. "You're right. I don't believe you."

I should have saved my breath, but I plowed on. "That's not all I saw. A man came out of the sea. From the U-boat. He's got to be a German. Not just any German. A German spy!"

Howard frowned.

"I'm telling you, a German spy landed on our beach. He had some kind of crate or chest. It looked heavy. He had to carry it on his shoulder."

Howard's eyes narrowed. "Just because you messed up in the game and dropped like a fly in the spelling bee is no reason to make up some dumb story. You just want to look like a big shot."

I jumped in front of him, blocking his way. Who did he think he was, calling me a liar? "I'm not making it up. I *saw* the sub! *And* the spy!"

"Save your crazy stories for the comic books," Howard said. He shoved me out of his way. I shoved him back.

Mr. Jolly stepped in between us. "Gentlemen, cease and desist this instant." I glared at Howard. He glared back. "Big Mouth's telling lies again," Howard said.

Mr Jolly didn't even give me a chance to say anything. He took my arm. "Frank, my boy, we need to have a little talk." He led me back to the classroom.

"Listen, Mr. Jolly, I saw something last night that I could hardly believe myself." And I told him what I'd told Howard.

He nodded his head a few times as he heard me out. When I finished, Mr. Jolly cleared his throat. "Frank, we both know you have a talent for relating, umm, shall we say, imaginative tales. This spy story sounds a bit like one of them. You appear to be a fine young man who hardly needs to make up tales."

"Honest, Mr. Jolly. It's the truth."

"Sounds more like a bad dream to me. I suggest you forget it."

I pulled at my knuckles. *Pop!* Mr. Jolly glared at me. I shoved my hands in my pockets. "It wasn't a dream," I said. "It really happened. I wouldn't make up a thing like that. You have to believe me. There's a spy or maybe a saboteur loose in this town."

"Enough of this nonsense, Frank. Do I have your word that this is the end of this wild tale?"

I squared my shoulders. "No, sir, Mr. Jolly, I couldn't do that."

"Very well." He bent over his desk and scribbled a note. "Take this to Mr. Moore."

I stomped down to the principal's office, handed him the note, and repeated my story. "This is a very serious matter," he said. "Why didn't you come directly to me or to the authorities?"

It was true I'd wanted to impress the guys, but I wasn't about to admit that. "I planned to tell my mom. I figured she'd know what to do."

"Yes, and did you tell your mother?"

"No, sir. But only because she was asleep."

Mr. Moore drummed a pencil on his desk. "And you didn't think it important enough to wake her?"

I tried to explain, but Mr. Moore rose from his chair, placed his ham-size hands on his desk, and leaned toward me. "Frank, in wartime we must be vigilant. But our military would never allow a spy to slip through their net of security. They are ever on the alert, constantly patrolling our shores."

"Yes, sir, that's what my dad did before he shipped out. But Mr. Jolly told us about the tanker that got blown up by a U-boat right off the coast. He said the flames lit up the sky for miles. If they could do that, I don't see why they couldn't drop off a spy."

"True. We did have that terrible mishap, but to suggest that an enemy submarine succeeded in making its way to our shore and delivered a spy onto our beach is beyond belief. I forbid you to speak of this matter in these hallowed halls or anywhere else on the school grounds."

I gave up. But there was no way I could forget what I saw. No way I could pretend it didn't happen. Mom would believe me; then we'd see some action.

The last bell rang, and with it a bell went off in my head. Why hadn't I thought of it before? I turned to Howard before he could escape. "Hey, Howard, you want in on the proof of my spy?"

Howard snorted. "Sure thing. Lead me to him."

"No kidding. I told you the spy buried something in the sand. All I have to do is show you where. You can be my witness when I dig it up." That stopped Howard dead in his tracks. No way could he resist being in on the scoop of the year. "When's that?" he asked.

"Soon as I get home."

I could see Howard struggling to act nonchalant, like the biggest war story Jacksonville had ever seen wasn't about to break wide open. His lower lip twitched to shoot out. His thumb jerked back and forth.

"Since you need a witness..." He yawned and tried to

look like he was doing me a favor. "…I guess I could pedal over."

"Bring a shovel," I said as I ran for my bus.

I clambered up the front steps. "Mom! Mom! I've got something important to tell you."

"Not as important as my news," Mom said, waving a piece of V-mail in my face.

I tried to grab the letter, but Mom wasn't about to let go. So I threw my books on the table and pulled up a chair beside her. "Is it really a letter from Pops? What's it say?" The spy would have to wait.

"Pops sent the letter to our old address. Uncle Norm forwarded it." Mom smoothed the letter out on the table so I could see. She began reading it out loud.

> *Dear Edie,*
>
> *I trust you received my telegram telling you not to come to Florida.*

"We didn't get a telegram, did we, Mom?"
Mom shook her head and kept reading.

> *I tried to telephone, but the guys were lined up halfway around the block waiting to use our one and only pay phone. I completed gunnery school two days before you were to leave for Florida. I hope you're not too mad at me for not telling you about the school. I never dreamed we'd leave Jacksonville so fast. We sailed on ▮▮▮▮▮▮▮▮▮▮▮▮▮▮▮▮▮▮▮▮▮▮▮▮▮ This is the real thing, if you know what I mean. As I write this we are near ▮▮▮▮▮ not too far from where Grandma was born.*

Mom and I grinned and smacked our right hands together. "Ireland!" we shouted. "Near Dublin," added Mom.

"Wow, isn't Pops swell? He slipped in his whereabouts right under the censor's nose. All that blanking out didn't do them any good."

"But it keeps the enemy from knowing his ship's whereabouts, and that's the important thing." Mom went back to the letter.

> *Don't work too hard, Edie. It may be* ▮▮▮ ▮▮▮▮▮▮▮ *I return. Wait for me. I love you and Francis too. Tell Francis he'll have to be the man around the house a while longer. Keep the faith.*
>
> *Love and kisses,*
> *Ted*

Mom and I sat at the table grinning at each other, letting Pops' words settle over us like a warm blanket.

After a while Mom sighed. She reached over and squeezed my hand. "What's your news, Francis?"

"Oh my gosh, I almost forgot. Last night when I was down at the beach…"

"At night?" Mom's eyebrows rose like antennae. "What were you doing on the beach at night?"

"Just looking at the stars. But that's nothing. Wait till you hear what I saw." And I told Mom the same story I'd been telling all day long.

At first she looked surprised, then worried. But when I finished, she burst out laughing. "Oh, Francis, you are the most wonderful storyteller. Just like Pops. You almost had me fooled."

I slumped in my chair. Mom kept talking, telling me

Pops would get a big kick out of the story and on and on. But I stopped listening. What was wrong with everybody? Why didn't anyone believe me?

Well, I'd get the proof. Just wait till they saw it. I rubbed my hands together and nearly laughed out loud thinking about the expression on everyone's face when I produced the spy's chest full of who knows what.

"Hollahan." It was Howard at the screen door with his hair wild and sticking up like a red top hat, making him look a good head taller. I invited him in and introduced him to Mom.

"It's so nice to meet one of Francis' little friends," Mom said. I winced twice. Once at the Francis. Again at the little friend, who towered over Mom.

"Gotta get going, Mom," I said, pushing Howard back out the door. "We'll bring back proof of the spy."

"Isn't that nice," Mom said. She smiled a sweet little smile as if she were indulging two toddlers. "Run along then and have your adventure."

I led the way to the beach with Howard mumbling, "So your mom doesn't believe you, either. This had better be good, Hollahan."

7

Found and Lost

Howard and I hit the beach at the same time. Waves crashed on the shore, and a gusty wind stung us with driven sand. I charged ahead to the high-tide mark. Following the line of washed-up seaweed, I walked north. Howard kept up with me. "So where's the spy stuff?" he asked.

"Huh?" I asked, holding my hand to my ear.

"Where's the spy stuff?" he shouted.

I cupped my hands around my mouth. "Look for footprints. They'll lead us straight to the spot." We walked back and forth, studying the sand. The only prints we saw were our own.

"Doggone, the storm must have washed them away," I muttered. The wind-driven sand had already half-filled our footprints. I gave my thumb knuckle a good crack. I walked back to the dunes to get my bearings. Howard was right behind me. "Let's see. I was here. The man came out of the ocean about there."

"Quit stalling, Hollahan."

"Things look different in the daylight." I filled my lungs and gave it my best guess. "Over there, by that clump of palmettos."

I grabbed a stick and began poking the sand. Howard leaned on his shovel and watched. Pretty soon there were more holes in the sand than in a tennis net.

"I know it's here somewhere," I muttered.

"Yeah, yeah," Howard said.

I kept poking.

Howard hefted the shovel onto his shoulder. "I've got better things to do," he said. "See you around."

Just then my stick struck something hard. "Yowee!" I cried. "I found it."

Howard spun around and came running back. "You sure?" he asked, pushing the shovel into the sand.

"Sure as sugar comes from cane," I answered. I shoved Howard aside. Down on my hands and knees, I scooped up handfuls of sand and tossed them aside. Too slow. I dug like a dog, my arms going like sixty, the sand flying out between my legs. Hot dog! Something hard and smooth. I cleared away more sand. "Here it is!" I shouted.

Howard leaned over my shoulder as I ran my hand across the smooth, dark surface. Howard jumped back. "Whew! What's that stink?"

I'd been too busy digging to notice. Until now. An awful stench rose from the ground. I gagged and choked back my lunch. Holding my nose with one hand, I cleared away more sand. Howard shoveled it to one side. The dark-colored surface grew bigger. And bigger. Pretty soon it was twice the size of any chest.

"Holy cow!" Howard exclaimed. "It's a giant sea turtle, dead and buried. And it's been here for a *loooong* time."

I peered into the hole. By golly, it did have that squared look of a turtle shell. "How did a sea turtle get buried here?"

"Aw, dead ones wash up on the shore sometimes, and the city's bulldozer buries them on the spot." Howard's thumbs turned down. "Some chest, Hollahan."

"Okay, so I got the wrong place. Maybe it's over by those palmettos," I said, pointing to another clump farther up the beach.

"You and your phony baloney! You're as crazy as Weird Wanda. As though one nut on this beach isn't enough. Now there are *two* of you! I have better things to do than dig up the whole doggone beach." Howard took his shovel and left.

Who the heck was Weird Wanda? I covered the dead turtle with sand and threw myself down in the sea oats. My arms felt like dead weight. My legs were wobbly. Sweat poured off me. I sprawled on my back and let the cold December wind blowing off the whitecaps sweep over me. I gulped in the salt air and watched the seagulls dip and glide across the gray skies. Their calls were the only sound I heard above the pounding surf. I closed my eyes and tried to get a clearer picture of the night before.

The next thing I knew, something warm, wet, and rough slouched across my face. My eyes flew open. With a yelp I bolted upright. Something brown and furry flung itself at my chest. I threw my arms up to protect my face, but a wet nose nudged them aside. I pushed away my tormentor and got a good look. It was nothing but a wavy-haired spaniel. The dog's stubby tail whipped the air with a definite statement of friendliness.

"Hey there, pooch," I said, stroking his head, trying to settle him down. "Where did you come from?" I looked around. Gulp! Coming along the beach in my direction was an honest-to-goodness giant. He was bundled in an old trench coat and scruffy army boots. A cap was pulled low on his forehead.

The hair stood up on the back of my neck. "*Spy!*" my brain waves screamed. I hunkered down and slipped behind the bushes. My new pal bounded after me and tugged at my sleeve, begging me to play. "Go away," I whispered, pushing the dog aside while I kept an eye on the man getting closer by the second. Finally, the dog bounded toward the stranger. The man jerked his head up and the wind sent his cap flying.

I blinked. Twice. He was a she! No spy. Only a girl. A giant of a girl, but only a girl. The breath swooshed out of me like a popped balloon. What a relief!

She chased her hat and suddenly was very close to me. I took a good look. This girl could have joined Mr. Jolly in the circus. She could be in the sideshow as the Giant of Jacksonville Beach. I couldn't tell how old she was, but I'd guess not long out of high school. With her cap gone, her dark hair hung loose to her waist, much longer than girls usually wore their hair. Could this be the Weird Wanda Howard had just compared me to?

Wanda or whoever she was stooped down to pat the dog. I couldn't hear what she was saying because of the wind and the surf, but I could see her lips move. She tossed a stick, and the dog charged after it.

I stood up. "Hey!" I called. She looked right at me. One eye was blue, the other brown. Weird. But right off, I knew I liked the blue eye better. I waved. She ducked her head, jumped up, and turned back in the direction she had come.

"Wait up!" I shouted. She broke into a run. "Hey, I only want to ask you a question." But she turned inland and disappeared behind the sand dunes. Strange, very strange. I wondered if she knew about the spy. Maybe he was holding her captive. Naw, not that giant. Besides, she wouldn't be walking the beach if she were his prisoner. Maybe she was in cahoots with the spy. Maybe that's why she ran.

I took off after her. Her footprints led me to a small house shaded by huge oaks and pretty well hidden behind a tall, thick hedge. I could have walked right past without even seeing it. A great hideout for a spy. I pushed aside some branches and crept closer. An open porch ran across the front of the house. On one side was a small victory garden of squash, winter beans, carrots, and a few scraggly tomatoes still clinging to leafless vines. On the other side, bushes grew right up to the house.

I sneaked closer. Going from window to window, I peered in. Everything was neat as a pin, plain and simple. One room reminded me of the science lab at school, with a long table and lots of test tubes and jars. A chemistry chart hung on the wall. Very interesting. I moved on and found the girl in the kitchen pulling down a glass from the cabinet. She was alone.

Taking a deep breath, I knocked on the kitchen window. The back door flew open like she was waiting for me. I jumped back. She held her spaniel by the collar. The pooch that had been licking my face in a frenzy of affection minutes ago didn't look any too friendly now.

"W… W… What do you want?" the girl asked.

"I have a question," I said, taking a step toward her. Pooch strained at his collar and growled. I backed up and nearly tripped over a watering can.

"G… G… Go away," the girl said. She slammed the door.

Gee, all I wanted to do was ask if she'd seen a stranger. I headed back, kicking the sand and grumbling about rude people. I wished I'd never seen that Nazi spy or the gigantic girl.

When I came near to where I'd been digging, I picked up the stick and poked around by the other palmettos. Nothing. But as I turned to leave, something caught my eye. I pulled a piece of heavy gray paper from between two sharp-edged palm leaves. Red ran along a crease and smeared one side of the paper. Blood! At least it sure looked like blood. Maybe the blood of the spy!

Very carefully, I opened the paper that was still damp from last night's rain. The numbers "1-12-43" were scrawled across the top. Directly below were a dozen other number combinations. I stared at them, puzzling over their meaning. Could they be dates? The number "one" could stand for January, the "twelve" for the day of the month, and the "forty-three" for 1943. I ran my finger down the column: "14-12-43" popped up halfway down. That shot down my date theory. I never heard of a fourteenth month.

I stood there scratching my head. Every single combination had a twelve in the middle. Very strange. Then it hit me like a monster wave. If this paper belonged to the German spy, then the dates would be written the European way. They put the day first and then the month. All those twelves could stand for December.

I checked the first date again. "1-12-43." If I was right, that would be the first of December, 1943. Yesterday's date. Hey, that's the day the spy landed! I'll bet this paper belonged to him. This must be his blood. Wow!

I made a mad dash for home. Bolting through the door, I waved the paper in Mom's face. "Look, proof the spy was on the beach." The red streak paled to a faded pink in the lamplight, but the numbers were clear.

"Good heavens, Francis, that paper could have come from anywhere at any time."

"But, Mom, nobody comes to this beach. Not this time of year. Besides, it has Wednesday's date on it. And look here. That's blood, the spy's blood. He must have cut himself on the palmettos."

Mom tied her apron around her waist. "You and your imagination, Francis. I wish you'd stop talking about spies. You're starting to give me the willies. Enough is enough."

Mom snatched the paper out of my hand and tossed it in the trash.

As soon as she left the room, I retrieved the paper. I didn't care what Mom said; I knew that paper was connected to the spy.

8

Gathering Moss

Saturday morning, as I wolfed down cornflakes and grapes, a truck screeched on the gravel in front of the house. Doors slammed, and a dozen voices called back and forth. Howard jumped off the flatbed of a battered pickup truck. What the heck was he doing here? Then I saw other kids from our class. They fanned out in all directions and started pulling down the wispy gray beards of Spanish moss that hung in the live oaks. I tore out the door and bolted down the steps. "Hey, what's going on?"

Joey walked toward the truck with an armful of moss. "We're decorating the cafeteria. It's the big Sadie Hawkins Day dance tonight. It'll look really swell with this Spanish moss draped from the hoops and the rafters."

"Good idea," I said, as if I knew what he was talking about. The dance was news to me. "Uh, who's Sadie Hawkins?" I asked.

"Don't you guys from Philly know anything? Sadie Hawkins is when the girls ask the guys, like in the comic strip *Li'l Abner*. Guess that means you're not going?"

"Never can tell," I said.

"Maybe you'll get lucky. I know one person who's interested." Joey pushed aside some moss, scratched his chin, and nodded toward the road. "Here comes your ticket now."

Butterscotch Eyes, her yellow hair all windblown, her cheeks red from the cold, pedaled up the road on a boy's bike ten sizes too big for her. She wobbled around mud puddles left from Friday night's rain. When she spied Joey and me, she slammed on her brakes and skidded to a stop. The bike tipped to the side. I pictured Rosemarie landing in the gravel, flattened beneath the monster bike. I jumped to her rescue and steadied the monster. Rosemarie smiled. Boy, did I love that little gap between her teeth. She swung her leg over the back fender in a vision of pure grace and beauty. My heart flipped.

I must have had a dippy look on my face, because Joey nudged me with his elbow and snickered. "Boy, have you got it bad." He hunched his shoulders, bobbed around on the soles of his feet, and jabbed at me with his free hand, like a sparring prizefighter.

Rosemarie propped her bike against a tree. "Hey, Joey. Hey, Frank," she said in that soft Southern drawl I was growing to like.

"H…" Nothing came out. I tried again. "Hi, uh, Rosemarie."

"Did y'all leave any moss for me?" she asked, twirling a strand of hair around her finger.

"We're just getting started," Joey answered. He headed for the truck. Rosemarie started to follow him.

I thought quickly. "How about helping me with that tree?" I pointed in the opposite direction. "I'll climb up and toss the moss down to you."

"Okay."

"Are you goin' to the dance?" Rosemarie asked, as I grabbed a sturdy branch and pulled myself up into the tree.

What kind of way was that to invite a guy to a dance? I

sure wasn't going to admit no one had asked me. "Naw, I don't dance."

"Oh," she said. "Well, you don't have to dance. Not everyone dances. You could just hang out and talk and have refreshments."

"That's true," I said, tossing down an armful of Spanish moss.

"Would you… ?" she began.

"What?" I asked. I was all set to say yes. I'd go anywhere in the world with Rosemarie.

"Ouch!" Rosemarie slapped her arm. "Something bit me."

"Watch out for the moss. It's buggy. Probably chiggers. They get under your skin and drive you crazy. Now, what were you saying?"

"Oh, nothin'," she said. And darned if she didn't change the subject. "Guess who called me last night?" She didn't wait for an answer. "Gladys. She told me what happened at the beach yesterday."

"How does she know?"

"Joey told her."

"Joey wasn't there."

Rosemarie heaved a sigh. "Lloyd told Joey."

"Lloyd wasn't there either." This conversation was getting nowhere.

"Well, Gladys said that Joey said that Lloyd said that Howard told him everything." Rosemarie dragged out the last word, *everything*, like it was some big deal.

I growled and ground my teeth. Darn Howard, blabbing all over the place. "What exactly did you hear?" I asked, none too politely.

"Just that y'all went huntin' for some kind of chest the spy buried. He said you didn't find it. I guess you know that Howard's more convinced than ever that you made up the whole spy story."

I could feel the steam coming out of my ears. "Yeah, and what do you think?"

Rosemarie stood under the tree, her arms spread wide, waiting to catch the next batch of Spanish moss. "Oh, I believe you, Frank." She looked up at me with those butterscotch eyes and the most earnest expression I'd ever seen.

Wow! I darn near fell out of the tree. "Really?" I croaked. I didn't realize how hopeless I'd felt until then. I cleared my throat. "I'll let you in on a secret, Rosemarie. After Howard left yesterday, I found something in the dunes." I swung down from the tree. "Wait here. I'll show you."

I dashed inside and felt around under my mattress until I came up with my super clue. I held it up to the light. What? I couldn't believe my eyes. The bloodstain looked even paler than I remembered, almost like it wasn't there at all. I couldn't show it to Rosemarie like that. I cracked my knuckles, stuffed three sticks of gum in my mouth, and thought.

I don't know what possessed me. I became a madman. I rushed into the kitchen, got down the ketchup bottle, unscrewed the top, stuck my finger in the ketchup, and smeared it across the paper. I smudged up the red streak until it looked the way a fresh bloody smear should look. Satisfied, I presented my super clue to Rosemarie.

"Oh, my gosh. It's blood," Rosemarie gasped.

Yep, my genius paid off. "But that's not all. Open it."

Rosemarie peeled back the thick paper and read off the numbers. She shrugged her shoulders. "What do they mean?"

"They're dates. The first one is the day the spy landed."

"What about the others?"

"I don't know yet. Maybe more spies are landing."

"Oh." Her eyes grew big. "Oh," she said again. "I'll bet Howard will believe you when he sees this."

Gee, that's the last thing I wanted. As luck would have it, Howard and Joey rounded the corner at that exact moment, swatting at their arms like they were being attacked. Rosemarie waved the paper in Howard's face. "Ha-ha. Proof that Frank saw a spy. See. The spy's blood. And it has the date he landed and more dates too. Frank found it on the beach."

"Give me that," Howard said, snatching the paper out of her hand. He flipped it from front to back. "Anybody could have written this. You wrote it, didn't you, Frank?"

"No. Look at the way the sevens are crossed. Americans don't write sevens like that. That's the way they write in…"—I paused for the full effect—"…Germany. It's the European way. And another thing, they always put the day of the week before the month, just like these dates are written."

"Who says?"

"My pop, that's who. Besides, I've seen it in letters from my Irish cousins."

Howard snorted. "If you know that fancy way to write sevens, then, like I said, you could have written it."

Rosemarie stood right up to him. "What about the blood? Huh?" She jabbed her finger in his chest. "Huh? Explain that."

Howard didn't budge. "I'll bet it's cherry juice. Or ketchup."

My stomach lurched from here to Philly. I tried to keep from turning gray by gulping oxygen. "You wouldn't believe your own grandmother on Christmas," I said, lunging for the paper.

Howard jerked it away. He held the note up to his nose.

"By golly, it is ketchup. You tripped yourself up good this time, Frank. Nobody will believe you now."

Howard wadded up the paper. "Hey, Joey! Catch." My one and only clue flew through the air as Joey and I charged after it. The crumpled note landed in a mud puddle. Joey got there first, scooped it up, and lofted the wet wad back to Howard. Rosemarie kicked Howard in the shins. He laughed, tore off a piece of the paper, and tossed it in her direction. He pitched the rest to Lloyd, who stood in the street pounding his fist into his palm and shouting, "Over here."

Two against three. Rosemarie and I looked like Mexican jumping beans, trying to snag my evidence. The paper fell in puddles more times than I could count. With each toss the wad shrunk, pieces of it mashed to pulp. Finally, I grappled what was left away from Lloyd—and only then because he stopped to scratch his ear.

"Face it, Frankie Baby," Howard said. "There isn't any spy. There never was a spy. There never will be a spy." He motioned to Lloyd and Joey. "Come on, let's finish this job and get out of here. My brother's tired of waiting around. He's got places to go with his truck." The three of them walked off, Joey scratching his nose, Frank his elbow, and Lloyd his stomach.

I hoped the chiggers would eat 'em alive.

I tried to smooth out what was left of the paper on the porch railing. Nothing. The dates were totally destroyed. Good thing I'd memorized at least some of them. I stuffed what was left in my pocket and slumped against the post.

"Was that really ketchup on the paper?" Rosemarie asked.

Gee, why did she have to bring that up? The last thing I wanted to do was admit that I'd pulled such a dumb stunt.

But Pops always said the best way out when you've done something stupid is to tell the truth. So I did. I explained where I'd found the paper, how the bloody streak faded, how I was only trying to make the streak look the way it probably had before it got rained on and half washed off. I swore it all on a stack of Mom's best pancakes that everything else I said was on the up and up.

Rosemarie looked down at her hands. She fiddled with her fingernails for a long time. "That wasn't very smart," she murmured.

"Dumbest thing I ever did," I said, kicking the bottom step. I figured it was bye, bye, Rosemarie. She'd hop on her bike and ride out of my life forever.

Finally, Rosemarie raised her head. "Do you think that chest is still buried on the beach?"

Woowee! What a break! Rosemarie believed me. She sure was swell. "Stick with me, Rosemarie. There's a spy somewhere out there, and I intend to prove it."

"How?"

"Well, I'm glad you mentioned the chest," I said. "I've been thinking a lot about that. If the spy found a place to hide nearby, he could have come back and dug up the case while it was still raining. So the footprints would have washed away. The problem is that there's no good place to hide around here."

Rosemarie's eyes flew open. "Weird Wanda's!"

"Huh?"

"The spy could be hidin' at Weird Wanda's, I mean Wanda Barr's house. You can't even see the house from the road, and she practically lives on the beach. It would be a perfect hideout."

I scratched my head. "By any chance is this Wanda a giant?"

"Well, she is pretty big," Rosemarie said.

"One eye brown, the other blue?"

Rosemarie nodded.

I popped my gum. "That's who I saw on the beach yesterday. And you're right about her house making a great hideout. But the only one hiding out there is Weird Wanda. I know because I followed her. No sign of a spy. She was alone. And not friendly! She slammed the door in my face."

"She won't talk to anyone," Rosemarie said, shrugging her shoulders. "Because of that, and those wild outfits she wears, people call her weird. When she does go into town, which is rare, she hands the salespeople her shopping list so she won't have to say anything. My mother says it's because she stutters so bad."

Wanda sounded weirder by the minute. "What else do you know about her?" I asked.

Rosemarie sat down on the porch step and cupped her chin in her hand. "She lives alone except for her dog. She takes him everywhere she goes. Her parents died a couple of years ago in an automobile accident, and her brother's off fightin' in the Pacific. He and my brother Jim are good friends. They both joined the Navy right after Pearl Harbor."

Rosemarie grew quiet like she was thinking about her brother and his friend. Then she went on. "Wanda dropped out of school when she turned sixteen. That was right after her brother left. They say she never opened her mouth in class but was a genius in chem lab."

"That explains all those test tubes and stuff I saw at her house." I leaned on the rail. "With your brothers being friends, does Wanda speak to you?"

"She smiles at me when we meet on the street. But that's all."

"Getting back to the spy," I said, "I sure wish there was some way I could find out if Wanda's seen any strangers since Wednesday."

Rosemarie clasped her hands together under her chin. For a minute there I thought she was praying. Then she threw her hands open. "What are we waitin' for? Let's go talk to Wanda. If I'm with you, maybe she'll let us in."

"Yeah, that might work. Maybe she'll listen to me if she sees someone she knows. And she doesn't have to talk. She can write down whatever she knows. That's all I'll ask."

9

Contact

Rosemarie and I topped the last dune. We stopped and filled our lungs with the briny gusts blowing in from the sea. The ocean was still rough from yesterday's storm, and the wind billowed our clothes like sails. It sure felt good standing there in the sun with Rosemarie beside me.

I tapped Rosemarie's arm and pointed to a clump of broken shells at the high-tide mark. I leaned close so she could hear me over the sound of the wind and sea. "See, there's where the spy came ashore. He buried the chest up near the dunes. You can see where I flattened out the sand when I covered up the turtle. And the paper I showed you was stuck in this palmetto bush." I kicked the sand, spraying the bush. "These palmetto blades are pretty sharp. I figure the spy cut himself on one."

Rosemarie nodded, her butterscotch eyes turning dark and serious. "I'll bet you're right, Frank."

The tall sea grass whipped and stung our legs as we ran down the dune and onto the beach. My arm bumped Rosemarie, and the next thing I knew we were holding hands. I pretended it was the most natural thing in the world and kept on talking. "Yep, I'm pretty sure the spy dug up the chest. But I figure he's hiding out somewhere close by."

Rosemarie sucked in her breath and gripped my hand tighter.

"It's okay," I said. "You're safe with me."

Her hand relaxed. "Let's talk about somethin' else," she said. "Like the Sadie Hawkins dance. Will you..." Her voice dropped and she mumbled something, but I couldn't hear.

"Will I what?"

She ducked her head and spoke real fast. "Will you go to the dance with me?"

"You bet!" I said. I plucked a seashell off the beach and flung it as far as I could into the ocean. I would have done a little jig like Pops does when he's really happy, but then I would have had to let go of Rosemarie's hand. I sure didn't want to do that.

We walked on up the beach really slowly, talking and kicking at the shells. I forgot about Wanda. If a submarine had beached itself right in front of us, I doubt I would have noticed. I could have kept on walking clear to Philadelphia.

But not Rosemarie. I guess she's one of those people who's easily distracted. We hadn't gone twenty yards when she stopped and tilted her head. "Did you hear that?" she asked. "Look over there."

I followed her pointing finger. Farther up the beach, Wanda the Giant stood at the shoreline, her hands cupped around her mouth. All her words were going out to sea.

The wind shifted, and I heard her shouts but couldn't make out the words. Breaking waves raced across the sand and splashed over her boots. Instead of backing away, she waded in deeper and kept yelling at the ocean.

Rosemarie and I looked at each other. "Weird is right," I said. "There's nothing out there but the sea, the sky, and a couple of screeching sea gulls. I think she's gone around the bend."

Weird Wanda paced back and forth in water swirling around her knees. I followed her gaze, and, for a second, I thought I saw something bobbing in the ocean. But with the sunlight dancing on the waves, I figured it was my imagination.

Rosemarie dropped my hand and shielded her eyes against the brightness. "It's Wanda's dog, Juniper," she said. "He's awfully far out."

Wanda kept shouting and waving her arms. Finally, I saw the dog. He had turned toward shore.

"Oh, Frank," Rosemarie said, clutching her hands to her chest. "Juniper's paddlin' so hard against the current, but he's not gettin' anywhere." Just then a wave washed over the pup's head. A second later, another. Rosemarie looked faint. "Poor Juniper. His big, floppy ears are draggin' him under. Oh, Frank, he's goin' to drown!"

Rosemarie broke into a run. I followed. The sand sucked at our feet and flew off our heels. As we reached Wanda, she turned, and I saw tears in her eyes and fear on her face. "R... R... Riptide," she blurted out. Juniper struggled on, more often under the crests than over. Wanda bent down through the surf and tugged at her boots.

Rosemarie looked horror-stricken. She leaned toward me and whispered, "Wanda's a terrible swimmer."

I looked at Wanda. I looked at Rosemarie. And I looked at Juniper. What's a guy to do? I kicked off my shoes, ripped off my jacket and shirt, and headed for the water.

"Don't!" screamed Rosemarie. "The riptide will get you too."

I ignored her warning and plunged into the breakers. Forget what people say about the Gulf Stream being warm. The cold stabbed through me like a knife. Then the riptide caught me. I didn't resist. I had to get to Juniper fast. It didn't take long for us to meet.

I grabbed at Juniper's collar, but his eyes went wild and his sharp claws raked my arm. I tried again, all the while feeling the current pulling us farther out to sea. I struggled toward Juniper for a third try and got a mouthful of salt water for my effort. My throat closed up. Gagging and spitting, I knew I had to get out of there fast.

"Come on, boy," I pleaded as I caught my breath and turned away. Instead of trying to buck the tide, I swam parallel to the beach, swimming across the current. Twenty strokes max, and I no longer felt the tide's strong pull. Juniper was right beside me. I could tell he felt the difference too, because the panic had left his eyes. He held his head high and paddled like a dog reborn. We turned toward shore and swam back together.

Wanda bounded into the surf and scooped Juniper into her arms. She wrapped him in her coat and nuzzled his neck as she plodded through the wet sand and on up the beach toward the dunes. She never even looked in my direction, as if I were nonexistent. I stared after her. Not one word of thanks. Not even a backward glance.

Shivering, I pulled on my clothes. I felt weak in the knees, partly from the cold and partly from the fear I'd ignored when I jumped into the ocean.

"You were wonderful, Frank," Rosemarie said with pure admiration in her eyes. "You were so brave. I don't know how you dared take a chance like that."

At least Rosemarie appreciated me. "Nothing to it," I said, trying to stop shaking. "It was just a little trick I learned."

Halfway to the dunes, Wanda turned. "T... T... Thank you."

"Wait up," I said, taking a step in her direction.

Wanda reared back, then got this closed-down look. Her eyes darted left and right. She dropped her chin and pulled her trench coat tight around both her and Juniper. "W... W... Why?"

Oops, not a good time to ask questions. I'd better say the right thing or she'd bolt. "I guess you already know Rosemarie," I said.

She nodded.

"My name's Frank. I live in the converted chicken coop across from Mr. Kinchloe's big house. You know the one I mean?"

Wanda bobbed her head. She wasn't talking, but at least she didn't run. "You can call me Chicken Coop Frank."

That got her. Her eyelashes fluttered like pale little butterflies. The corner of her mouth twitched like she wanted to smile but had forgotten how. "I... I... I'm Wanda."

"Well, Wanda, I saw something the other night I think you'd be interested in. It's a long story, but I'll make it quick 'cause I'm freezing."

Wanda seemed to notice my chattering teeth for the first time. "W... W... Would you like hot cocoa?"

Wow, an invitation! "I sure would."

"I'll help you make some," Rosemarie said, "if that's okay?"

Wanda and Rosemarie went in one direction, while I dashed home and changed into dry clothes. I jammed the stuff from the wet pants pockets into the dry ones, then trotted over to Wanda's.

Rosemarie, Wanda, and the cocoa were waiting. Steam rose from the cups sitting on the table. Juniper had been rubbed dry and lay on the couch with his chin resting on

Wanda's lap. Wanda scratched behind his ear and gave him little hugs. Rosemarie had settled at the other end and patted Juniper's hindquarters. I collapsed in the high-backed chair opposite the couch and reached for the cocoa.

I decided to play it cool and wait for Wanda to ask me what it was I thought she'd be interested in. I sipped the cocoa. "Hmm, good," I said, licking the chocolate from my upper lip. Wanda did the eyelash, lip-twitch thing. I waited.

Rosemarie fidgeted. I could tell she didn't like the silence. Finally the strain was too much for her. "Wasn't Frank brave?" she asked. She turned to me. "I know I told you before, Frank, but you were wonderful. How did you know what to do?"

Looking into Rosemarie's butterscotch eyes, I felt like the marshmallows melting in my hot chocolate. Then I glanced at Wanda. The shock of her two odd-colored eyes and fluttering lashes brought me back to reality.

"Pops is in the Navy," I told them. "He wrote me all about his training. I remembered what he said about riptides, that they could carry you out to sea. He said never fight the current by trying to swim against it, but swim across it. Worked just like Pops said."

Wanda rocked forward on the couch. Her face got chalky white. "Y… Y… Your dad sounds swell."

Wow, she was talking. Easy does it, I told myself. Don't scare her off. I told her about seeing the spy. I eased into the questions. "Have you seen a stranger around here?"

She shook her head no.

"Did you hear anything unusual Wednesday night around ten o'clock or later?"

Again, Wanda shook her head no. "B… B… But Juniper barked. A… A… A lot."

"But you didn't see anything?"

Wanda shrugged her shoulders. "I... I... I found a cigarette p... p... pack the next day." Wanda struggled hard,
trying to tell us something. Finally, she got enough out that
I realized she thought the pack of cigarettes was German.

"You mean 'cigarettes' was spelled with a z instead of a c?"
I asked, repeating what I thought she'd said.

Wanda's eyelashes fluttered. I took that for a yes.

That cinched it. This could be the break I needed. Who
would smoke German cigarettes but a German? "Where's
the pack?"

Wanda pointed to the fireplace.

"Oh, no," I cried, seeing nothing but ashes. "You
destroyed the evidence."

She blanched. "I... I... I... "

"It's okay," I flung over my shoulder as I grabbed the
poker and stabbed at the cold white ashes in the fireplace. I
got down on my hands and knees. Little by little, I swept
the ashes from one side to the other. Buried among them I
found a tiny scrap of aquamarine paper, blackened and
curled at the edge. About as much proof as my destroyed
bloody paper. Defeated, I sat back on my heels.

"Don't give up, Frank," Rosemarie said, slipping off the
couch and kneeling beside me.

I took a deep breath. "You're right, Rosemarie. There's a
spy lurking around here. People need to know, and I need
to prove it to them." I counted off on my fingers the things
I knew for certain. "First, there was the submarine. I heard
the throb of its engines, felt it in the ground, and smelled
the burned oil. Second, I saw the guy come out of the sea.
He dug a hole and buried something that looked like a
chest. Third, whatever he buried has disappeared." I pulled
at my knuckles. Wanda and Rosemarie stayed glued to the
couch and my every word. "Juniper went crazy barking the

same night the spy landed. And both Wanda and I found something the next morning. Yours, Wanda, was an empty aquamarine pack of cigarettes spelled with a *z*. No American cigarette pack that I know of is that color. And mine was a bloody piece of paper near the dig site with at least one significant date on it. The day of the landing."

Wanda made me stop and explain about the paper I found. Then I got back to the matter at hand. "Even though we can't place the spy here anytime after Wednesday night, I'll bet my collection of ship models that he's still around here. But where?" I paced back and forth. "Proof. I need good solid proof."

I stopped my pacing. "Cabanas!" I said, cracking my knuckles. "Since no one rents them in the winter for changing into swimsuits, it's the perfect hiding place."

Wanda nodded.

Rosemarie said, "Oh, Frank, you're so smart."

Hmm. I liked being recognized for my talents. "Maybe you two should stay here while I check out the cabanas. Things could get nasty."

"J...J...Juniper and I are going with you," Wanda said.

Rosemarie's eyes glistened, and she gulped a couple of times before jumping up. "Me too," she said.

Wanda handed each of us a marble bookend. "J...J...Just in case."

10

The Best Clue Yet

W anda, Rosemarie, and I crept over the dunes, keeping a sharp eye out for any activity. The wind had died down. Except for the steady rhythm of the waves breaking on the shore and the squish of the shifting sand beneath our feet, it was deadly quiet. When we neared the last dune, I motioned for Rosemarie and Wanda to wait. Wanda frowned but went along with my plan. She crouched down beside Rosemarie and clamped her hand over Juniper's mouth.

Running from one clump of palmettos to the next, I worked my way past the vacant parking lot to the rear of the cabanas. The afternoon sun bounced off the row of windows high on the whitewashed wall of the cabanas. A rickety sawhorse from who knows where leaned against the building. I dragged it under the first window and eased up on the crossbar. The top of my head barely reached the sill. Crusted salt-spray coated the glass. I licked my finger and ran it across the pane. Very slowly. Very carefully. If the spy saw me, I'd have to make a run for it. I held my breath and waited. No sound came from the cabana. I waited a second longer, then grabbed the sill and pulled myself up. I peered into the semidarkness.

A sink and toilet were partitioned off from the rest of the

room by gray wooden panels. The panels rose as high as the window but were open at the top. I could see the entire room in one quick glance. Empty as my coin bank.

I signaled thumbs down to Wanda and Rosemarie. I moved the sawhorse from window to window. Pretty much the same results all down the line, eleven cabanas so far. A few stored a clutter of beach chairs, fishing poles, beach balls, and floats, but no sign of life.

At the last one, I pressed my forehead against the window. Whoa, it moved. My heart pounded, but when I peered in, nothing. Putting my finger to my lips, I waved Rosemarie and Wanda over.

"I didn't see anyone," I whispered, "but I want to check inside this last one. Something tells me the spy's been here. I'll crawl through this loose window, where I figure he entered."

Wanda gave me a pitying look. "M... M... Maybe he went in the window, b... b... but I bet he came out the door."

"Right. Good thinking, Wanda." I wondered why I hadn't thought of that.

We walked around to the beach side, the side of the multicolored double doors. And sure enough, one lock dangled open, its looped latch gaping. Darkness oozed through the crack in the door. I tugged at one side. The hinges groaned in protest as the door opened out and caught in a sand drift. We squeezed through the narrow opening.

Once inside, we closed the door and waited for our eyes to adjust from the bright sunlight to the dim interior. Water dripped from the sink next to the toilet. A towel and woman's purple bathing suit hung on a hook, probably left behind by last summer's renters. Three folded beach chairs leaned against a wall, but a lounge chair sat open in the middle of the room.

"Very suspicious," I said.

Rosemarie tilted her nose in the air. "I smell stale cigarette smoke."

Juniper sniffed around the chair, then put his nose to the floor and circled the room twice. He trotted to the door, nudged it open, and took off down the beach like the Lone Ranger's speeding bullet. The three of us bolted after him.

When Juniper stopped, he was close to where I'd found the soggy paper. He buried his nose in the sand, wiggled it around, and came up snorting. He looked like a bandit with a sand mask. Sand flew out of his nostrils. His stubby tail wagged like sixty. Rosemarie giggled. I started laughing. Juniper's bandit face sure struck us as funny. We laughed so hard, we couldn't talk. Wanda stood over us with her hands on her hips. "W... W... What's so funny?" she demanded.

"Juniper's face," squealed Rosemarie and burst into another fit of laughter. Every time we tried to stop, Juniper snorted out sand or cocked his head or gave a yip, and off we'd go again. Wanda acted weird. One side of her mouth turned up like she wanted to laugh, but I think she must have forgotten how. By the time Rosemarie and I calmed down, Wanda had allowed herself a single "Ha!" and then just one more.

Juniper continued to bark and snort and dig. The next we knew, Juniper unearthed a small pouch wrapped in oilcloth and dropped it at Wanda's feet. Rosemarie and I crowded in close as Wanda peeled back the cover. Inside was a piece of paper. It looked familiar. The same rough linen as the one I'd found earlier, now all tattered and torn and wadded up in my pocket. I pulled it out. Despite its soggy state, we all agreed both papers came from the same writing tablet.

Rosemarie did the honors of unfolding our new find. It was blank.

I scratched my head. "What could be so important about a blank paper that someone would wrap it up to protect it from the weather?

"Maybe it has a secret message," Rosemarie said.

I looked at her like she was crazy. "There's nothing to see, so how can it be secret?"

Rosemarie bit her lip, like I'd hurt her feelings. "Well, once in school we made invisible ink. Maybe it's hidden like that."

Now there was a thought. "How did you make the ink?"

"It was easy," Rosemarie said. "We just dipped a feather point in onion juice and wrote our message. When it dried you couldn't see anything. Then when we held the paper up to a candle, the heat made our message visible."

"You know, Rosemarie, I think you might be on to something." I believe in giving credit where credit is due. "We should try it." I turned to Wanda. "How's your candle supply?"

Five minutes later, we were at Wanda's in the room where I'd seen all the test tubes. Now I got a really good look. Two long tables, each with a small sink, stands holding rows of test tubes, several Bunsen burners, large flasks for mixing formulas, and a great-looking microscope. The chemistry chart I'd seen the day I followed Wanda home was smudged with fingerprints from much use. Wow, I was impressed. I turned to Wanda. "What's all this for? Who uses it?" Wanda opened her mouth to speak, but all that came out was "M... M... M..."

Rosemarie came to her rescue. "Wanda's father was a pharmacist. He worked on making new medicines. Some of his medicines have been patented. Isn't that right, Wanda?"

Wanda smiled and nodded.

I noticed a book laying open on one of the lab tables. "Are you interested in this stuff?" I asked.

Wanda bobbed her head, and her face lit up like a sunrise.

"Mr. Jolly brags about you all the time, Wanda," Rosemarie said. "He calls you 'Wanda, the Science Wizard.' He says you're a genius."

Wanda blushed and left the room. She returned a minute later with a candle. Guess she thought we ought to get on with our own experiment.

"Can I try the candle first?" Rosemarie asked. Wanda lit the candle and handed it to Rosemarie, who held it behind the paper. "It only takes a minute," she said.

You could have heard a gnat hit the ceiling fan as the three of us stared at the paper, straining our eyes. I imagined letters and numbers magically materializing.

One minute passed. Two. "H... H... Hold it closer." Wanda said.

"But don't burn it!" I croaked.

We waited a while longer. Nothing. Wanda blew out the candle from four feet away. I was impressed. A giant puff from gigantic Wanda. "We'll have to try something else," she said. She spoke as easy and casually as Rosemarie. No stutter. That was a first. I started to say something, but then the stutter came back.

"D... D... Dad's chemistry books are on the top shelf."

For the first time, I noticed books lining three entire walls from floor to ceiling. Wanda climbed a stepladder and pulled down a dusty black text, *Chemical Formulary, Vol. VIII.* She blew off a thick layer of dust that swirled like a mini sandstorm. Laying the book on the table, she opened to page fifty-four and ran her finger down the first column. With Rosemarie on one side and me on the other, Wanda's finger stopped at a heading: *Invisible Ink*. Wanda pointed to the third formula.

I read out the ingredients needed to make a kind of ink other than onion juice visible. Wanda gathered the materials. She groped under a cabinet and retrieved an enormous glass jar. She poured in a cup of ammonia. Wow, the smell socked my nose and brought tears to my eyes. Rosemarie coughed and backed away. None of this bothered Wanda. She added a little water to the ammonia and slid the paper inside the jar. Before screwing on the lid, she clipped a string to the top of the paper to make certain it dangled above the liquid.

Rosemarie crossed her fingers. I snapped my gum. Wanda looked confident.

Rosemarie's lips parted. "Look," she whispered.

The three of us fell silent and watched as numbers and letters materialized. When I realized Rosemarie wasn't breathing, I nudged her with my elbow. She gulped in air and giggled with excitement. Letters took shape. Big, black, and bold! But the more I saw, the more confused I became. Rosemarie leaned forward. Squinting, I tried to make words of the letters.

"I... I... It's not English," Wanda said. "N... N... Not any language."

I pulled the paper from the jar and held it up so we could see better. "Nothing makes sense," I said. "It's just one long line after another of letters and numbers mixed together with no breaks for words." I read the first line, "G P 4 L M P 6 B P."

I chomped my gum twice, and it hit me. "Good gosh, it's in code!" Now that was exciting.

II

Breaking the Code

Wanda must have known we'd be no good working on empty stomachs. She fixed us peanut butter and jelly sandwiches and lemonade. After that, we set to work breaking the code. We tried using the numbers for letters. When that didn't work and we realized the highest number was seven, we tried assigning each number a day of the week. That looked promising for a while, but we couldn't arrange the letters around them to make sense.

Next, we counted each letter to see how many times it appeared. Wanda, the human abacus, beat Rosemarie and me by a mile. She pointed to her totals and Rosemarie read them out. "Fifty-three *p*s, twenty-one *d*s." And on down the list. "Since *e* is the most common letter in the alphabet, we'll change the *p*s to *e*s," I said. And we did. We tried all combinations of different letters in place of other letters or numbers.

Juniper woke up from his nap and padded over to the table. His front paws landed on the table with a soft thud. His eyes searched our papers as though he could read. Apparently he didn't like what he saw. He slumped back onto the floor with a sigh. Rosemarie must have felt the same way, because she slumped back into her chair with a sigh. "I give up, Frank. It's no use. No matter what we do, nothin' makes sense."

Wanda shrugged her shoulders. "M... M... Maybe it's in German."

I threw down my pencil in frustration. "Now you tell us."

"What else can we do?" Rosemarie asked, chewing on her pencil.

I started thinking out loud. "Okay, so we don't know what the message says. But it's still a swell clue that Juniper found." At the sound of his name, Juniper thumped his tail on the floor. I gave his head a pat and kept talking. "We know it's a coded message. That in itself should convince people there's a spy. But who to tell?" I got up and started pacing. "Not Mr. Jolly or the principal. They didn't believe me before, and I doubt they'll believe me now. And not my mom. She'd flip out." I gave my knuckles a good crack. "I've got it. I'll go to the police."

Rosemarie jumped up. "I'll go with you, Frank. I can back up your story."

"Great idea. In the meantime, we've got to keep this quiet. You saw how Howard and the guys treated the paper with the dates. I don't want anyone tampering with this evidence. We'll keep it our secret and save it for the police."

Wanda listened to our plan with her arms crossed and her eyelashes fluttering.

We made copies of the message and agreed that each of us would work on it at home on Sunday. I wrapped up the original and put it in my pocket.

"Don't forget, if any one of us figures it out, we'll let the others know right away. Agreed?"

Rosemarie and Wanda nodded. "When school lets out on Monday, Rosemarie, we'll go to the police. You can meet us there, Wanda." Wanda got her closed-down look, but I ignored it.

Rosemarie's hand flew to her mouth. "Oh, I forgot. I have

a piano lesson. Right after school."

"Gee, it's going to be hard enough to wait as it is. Can't you skip your lesson?"

Rosemarie pressed her lips together and solemnly shook her head. I cracked my knuckles and my gum in pure frustration. With her butterscotch eyes, Rosemarie pleaded for understanding. I calmed down.

"Then it's just you and me, Wanda. I'll meet you in front of the police station." Wanda's eyelashes went into fast flutter and sweat broke out on her upper lip. She shook her head so hard her hair slapped her face from one direction, then the other.

"I don't understand you, Wanda. You're the one who saw the cigarette pack. It was your dog, Juniper, that found the packet with the secret message." I picked up the formulary book. "And you're the one who figured out which formula to use to make the message visible. I'd think you'd want to be there when I talk to the police."

Wanda backed against the wall and kept shaking her head. "I... I... I can't."

What was happening? Everybody was backing out on me. "Why not?"

"Y... Y... You know."

"No, I don't have a clue."

"B... B... Because I s... s... stutter so b... b... bad."

I lashed out without thinking. "Boy, that's dumb. If your stuttering is keeping you from a simple thing like backing me up, what else is it keeping you from?"

"F... F... From going to c... c... college!" she spat out, her face red with anger. Juniper pushed between us, bared his teeth, and growled.

I backed away. "You're kidding, right?" But I saw she wasn't kidding at all. She looked miserable. Rosemarie glared at me from the doorway. I'd gone too far. Besides, I didn't like the way Juniper kept eyeing me. "I'm sorry," I said. And I meant it. I wished I hadn't badgered her. I wanted to take back everything and make things good again. "You're a brain, Wanda," I said. "No college would keep you out because you stutter."

"I'm thirsty," Rosemarie said. "Is it okay if I get a drink of water?" Wanda nodded absentmindedly and pointed toward the kitchen.

"Frank, help me reach the glasses," Rosemarie said, grabbing my hand and pulling me out of the room.

"I told you Wanda never finished high school," Rosemarie whispered, getting her own glass and turning on the tap. "And the only reason she didn't graduate is that everyone—no exceptions—has to take an oral exam. It's just part of the finals. That's why Wanda never graduated. She refused to try. No high school diploma, no college."

When we got back to the lab, Rosemarie announced that we had decided to wait until Tuesday to go together to the police. This was news to me, but all things considered, it sounded like a good idea. I fingered my copy of the code like I was thinking it over. "Yeah, that'll work," I said. Wanda looked relieved.

I gathered up the papers I'd been working on and started for the door. "I can trust you not to say anything to anyone, can't I, Wanda?"

She nodded.

"I sure hope Rosemarie and I can keep our mouths shut at school. It's going to be tough."

I turned to Rosemarie. "We have to keep our guard up, especially at the dance tonight. Okay?"

At the mention of the dance, Rosemarie glanced out the window. "Oh, my gosh, the sun's nearly down." She looked at her watch. "Eeek! It's after six. I'll have to ride my bike home in the dark. Mom's going to skin me alive."

"I'll go with you," I said.

Rosemarie bolted out the door. I charged after her. "Thanks, Wanda. See you later," I called over my shoulder as the screen door slammed behind me.

Rosemarie was so upset she outran me, which, considering the way I run, shouldn't have surprised me. As we came in sight of my house, Rosemarie cried, "My mother's car. Oh boy, oh boy, oh boy, am I in trouble."

Before we reached the steps, a wild woman burst out of the door. "Where have you been?" she screamed. She grabbed Rosemarie by the elbow. "Get in the car this minute."

"But my bike."

"Never mind your brother's bike. You won't be going anywhere for a long time. Maybe never."

"But the dance tonight."

"Dance? Are you out of your mind?"

Rosemarie gave me a pitiful look as her mother practically dragged her to the car. "I'm sorry, Frank," she said, fighting back tears. She must have felt awful. I know I would if my mom carried on like that.

"It's okay," I managed to say, but I don't think she heard me. Her mother was still yelling as she hustled Rosemarie into the car and slammed the door. When she came back around to the driver's side, she wagged her finger in my face. "And you. You stay away from my little girl."

I turned and looked at Mom, who stood in the doorway, not saying a word. When she saw me watching her, she motioned me inside.

"Gosh, Mom. I know we were late getting back, but Mrs. Twekenberry didn't have to go berserk. I don't mind taking the blame, but she sure embarrassed Rosemarie."

"Francis, things are worse than you realize. Mrs. Twekenberry received a telegram today from the War Department."

Oh, God, I didn't want to hear any more. But Mom put her hand on my shoulder and kept talking.

"Rosemarie's brother is missing in action, Francis. Mrs. Twekenberry is worried sick. I'm sure that's why she acted the way she did."

I eased down into a kitchen chair. A hard, tight knot gripped my stomach. Missing in action could easily mean killed in action. Mom didn't say any more, and I was glad. We both knew if it could happen to Rosemarie's brother, it could happen to Pops.

12

The Telegram

I fought my way through nightmares and tangled sheets to the smell of hot cinnamon teasing my nose. "Cookies for you to take to the Twekenberrys," Mom said when I stumbled into the kitchen. "I'd go with you, but I'm needed at the shipyard for a few hours."

"On Sunday?"

"Unfortunately, Francis, the war doesn't stop on Sundays, and neither does the war effort. There's barely enough time to get to church, but if we hurry we can make the nine o'clock service."

After church Mom boarded the bus for work. "Now, remember to take those cookies over to Rosemarie's and let them know we care."

I cared all right, but what was I going to say? It was too early to go now anyway. I'd think about it later. I went home and got out my copy of the coded paper. On the back, I'd written dates from the paper Howard had destroyed. It drove me nuts that I only remembered three. "December first." The day the spy landed. "December fifth." Hey, that was today. And "December seventh."

The dates faded away, and Rosemarie's image floated in my mind. I shook my head and tried to forget her and concentrate on the meaning of the dates. "December fifth." Could the Germans be landing another spy tonight? Or had they already landed one this morning before dawn? For all I knew, Jacksonville could be crawling with spies by now. On the other hand, the date could mean something else altogether. But what? A deadline to meet? A rendezvous date? I could only guess. I didn't have a clue.

I turned back to the hidden message and worked on breaking the code. But with this visit to Rosemarie's hanging over my head, I couldn't think straight.

At noon I gave up and stuffed my decoding notes into my pocket. I ate a raw hot dog, popped a couple of sticks of tutti-frutti in my mouth, covered the plate of cookies with wax paper, and headed for Rosemarie's.

I sure wasn't looking forward to this visit. For one thing, I wondered if Rosemarie's mother would let me in or if she would throw another hissy fit and send me packing. But worse than that, what could I say? Gee, what could anybody say at a time like this? I had plenty of time to think about it on my long walk into town. I tried a few phrases out loud, but most of the words stuck in my throat. Nothing sounded very good.

Rosemarie sat on her front steps with her chin in her hands, staring at the ground. Her eyes were swollen. She gave me a limp wave. I crossed the street, and we met by the bougainvillea hedge that bordered their property. Rosemarie kept her head down and plucked at the flowers.

I wanted to talk, but the words I'd practiced flew out of my head. I touched her hand. She didn't even look up. I cleared my throat. "Uh, Mom told me about your brother. I'm, uh, sorry."

Rosemarie sighed. "All my relatives came over to say the same thing. They're still here."

"Mom lit a candle in church this morning," I said, "and we said a prayer that everything would be okay."

"Thanks," Rosemarie murmured. "That's a lot nicer than our next-door neighbor." Rosemarie's head jerked up. Her eyes flashed. "That awful Mrs. Jones came over this morning. She brought a gold star. 'You might be needing this to hang in your window,' she said." Rosemarie made her voice sound all high and mighty. "Boy, can you believe her nerve?"

I shook my head no.

Rosemarie yanked off a leaf and shredded it into a zillion pieces. "A gold star in our window would tell the whole world someone in our family died in the war. Well, my brother Jim's not dead. He's not!"

I nodded my head as Rosemarie kept talking. "Mama got hysterical. Told Mrs. Jones to go home and mind her own business, that Jimmy was coming back. 'See that blue star,' Mama said." Rosemarie pointed to the blue star hanging in their front window, as her mother must have done with Mrs. Jones. "Mama looked Mrs. Jones right in the eye and set her straight. 'That blue star is going to stay right there, because our Jim is still serving his country.' And before Mama could stop herself, she said, 'Not like your 4-F Willard with his flat feet.'"

Rosemarie dropped her voice. "I think Mama regretted saying that about Willard being 4-F. Everyone knows how disappointed he was when they told him he couldn't join up and go fight. But Mama was hopping mad and couldn't help herself. Mrs. Jones stuck her nose in the air and said, 'It's not Willard's fault he has flat feet. He does a lot for the war effort. As for the gold star, my dear, I was only trying to help. You need to prepare yourself for the worst.'"

I figured maybe Mrs. Jones was right, but I couldn't tell Rosemarie that. I held out the plate of cookies. "Mom sent these. Want one?"

Rosemarie shook her head no, but she lifted the paper, took one, and nibbled at it anyway. She sighed. "Did you work on the code?" She asked it like she didn't really care—more like she thought she ought to make conversation.

"Not much," I said, juggling the plate of cookies as I slid my notebook out of my pocket. I showed her what I'd done. "It still doesn't make any sense."

Rosemarie shrugged her shoulders. "I read somewhere that spies double-code their messages."

"Gee, if that's the case, we'll never crack the code. It looks like we might have to leave the code-solving to the police."

Rosemarie's mouth dropped open, and her eyes grew big. She stared past me, her face chalky white. Gosh, I didn't think my plan was that bad. I turned and followed her gaze.

A skinny old guy wearing a Western Union cap wobbled past us on his bike. At the end of the Twekenberrys' front walk, he kicked down his bike stand and hobbled toward the house. He was holding a telegram in his hand. Oh, my gosh, it looked as if Rosemarie's family would need the gold star after all.

The two of us froze as the man shuffled up the steps to the porch. His hand shook as he rang the bell. It seemed forever before Mrs. Twekenberry came to the door. When she saw who it was, she stumbled backwards and had to grab hold of the door post to steady herself. Then we heard Mr. Twekenberry's voice from deep inside the house.

"Who is it, Lily?" When she didn't answer, Mr. Twekenberry came out and stepped to her side. His face never changed expression, but I saw a flicker of fear in his eyes. He took the telegram, slipped the old man some change, and murmured, "Thanks."

Mr. Twekenberry squeezed his wife's arm and stared at the telegram in his hand. He didn't rip the telegram open, just slowly turned the envelope over in his hand. He teased the flap open with his thumbnail, as though somehow it was important not to leave a ragged edge. My breath was choking me. I took Rosemarie's hand and she held on tight. We watched her father unfold the telegram and begin reading it to himself. Then, boy, did things speed up.

Mr. Twekenberry tossed the telegram in the air and threw his arms around Mrs. Twekenberry. He lifted all two hundred pounds of her right off the floor and spun her clear around in a circle. "Jimmy's alive!" he shouted. "They found our Jim. He's alive!"

I looked at Rosemarie. Her pale face flushed red. She smiled and laughed and couldn't stop. She clapped her hands, twirled around, and danced a silly jig right there in the front yard. Then she grabbed my hand and pulled me toward the house. The cookies scattered across the lawn, but who cared?

Mrs. Twekenberry, with tears running down her cheeks, bawled like a baby. Rosemarie's aunts and uncles and cousins all spilled out of the house and onto the porch. "What happened? Did you get news of Jim?" they asked. When they found out, they shouted and whooped and pounded each other on the back. They hugged Mr. Twekenberry, Mrs. Twekenberry, Rosemarie, and each other. In their excitement, they hugged me too. Even Rosemarie hugged me. And I hugged her right back. An uncle in loud suspenders got all choked up. When he talked, his voice cracked. He sounded like me and the other eighth-grade guys. After a while he just stood around and grinned, like me.

Mrs. Twekenberry dabbed at her tears and led the way back into the house. "Everybody come in. We're going to celebrate! Rosemarie, you and your friend make the coffee. Lucy, put the lace cloth on the table. Edgar, can you reach the sterling tea set on the high shelf? Millie, help me set out the good china."

"What a wonderful day. A glorious Sunday, indeed," Rosemarie's Aunt June said, as she joined Rosemarie and me in the kitchen. She squeezed Rosemarie's shoulder with one hand and threw open the refrigerator door with the other. Hauling out cream cheese, cucumbers, and a loaf of bread, she set to work making fancy little sandwiches. Cookies appeared out of nowhere, and Rosemarie cut apples into wedges and put them on a plate on the table. I carried the coffeepot into the dining room.

Everyone crowded around the table. Mr. Twekenberry raised a bottle of sherry in the air. "I was saving this for a special occasion. The only thing more special than this will be when Jimmy comes marching through that door, so today we celebrate." He poured the golden sherry into tiny glasses with slender stems. The light danced off the fancy cuts in the glass as he passed the sherry around the table. I didn't take one, but Mr. Twekenberry insisted, although he saw to it that Rosemarie and I received barely a thimbleful. "Just a sip," he said, "or you insult my son."

"To Jimmy," he said, raising his glass high. We all clinked our glasses together. Rosemarie smiled as she touched the edge of her glass to mine. I gave her a wink and she blushed. "Down the hatch," Mr. Twekenberry said. No problem. I figured I'd hardly taste it. I put the glass to my lips, threw my head back, and tossed down the sherry. It hit the back of my throat like a flaming match. My eyes nearly popped as the fiery liquid headed south, burning all the way down.

I was still gasping for air when it hit my stomach. I glanced at Rosemarie, who daintily sipped, then set her glass aside.

Finally, someone asked, "Exactly what did the telegram say?"

"Yes, where did they find Jim?" Aunt June asked. "Is he all right? Oh, dear, I hope he's not injured?"

Mr. Twekenberry struck his forehead with the heel of his hand. "The telegram! I tossed it away as soon as I saw Jimmy was found. I never finished reading it."

"Here it is, Papa," Rosemarie said, leaning across the table. "Frank picked it up on the way in and gave it to me."

Mr. Twekenberry took the telegram, put on his horn-rimmed glasses, and read it aloud.

> *We are pleased to inform you that your son, Radioman James Twekenberry, has been found alive.*

He looked up and grinned. "That's as far as I got. Now let's see what else is in here." He glanced back down at the telegram. "Ah, yes, here we are:

> *Radioman Twekenberry was wounded in action and treated at the field hospital. He will be sent to a hospital near his home for further treatment and recovery. You will be notified of specifics at a future date.*
>
> *Frank Knox, Secretary of the Navy, United States of America.*

"My Jimmy wounded?" Mrs. Twekenberry exclaimed, rising from the table.

"Now, Mama," Mr. Twekenberry said, giving her a hug.

"Our Jimmy is found. He's alive and he's coming home. For that, we'll be grateful. And we'll pray for the rest."

Rosemarie and I left the table and walked to the front door. "I think your brother's going to be okay," I said.

Rosemarie smiled. "I think you're right. I know my brother Jim. He'll fight hard to recover. He's a fighter like you are, Frank. Fights for what's important."

Wowed by the compliment, I nearly fell down the steps. "Thanks," I said.

"See you tomorrow in school," Rosemarie called after me.

13

Trouble at the Train Station

Mom walked in the door just as I finished rereading Pops' letters. He'd written every day, but they had arrived all at once. Yesterday, the mailman delivered five that Uncle Norm had forwarded from Philadelphia. Pops must not have received any of our letters, because he still didn't know Mom and I had moved to Florida. Any day now, he'd probably get a batch of letters from us.

"Mmm, Pops' letters," Mom said, bending over to kiss the top of my head.

"Aw, Mom," I said, ducking away, "I'm too old for that stuff."

She laughed and mussed my hair. "Did you figure out that word the censors blacked out?"

"I sure did. Pops was writing about the direction his ship was traveling. He knew that would clue us in as to where he is. He said he sighted land on the port side. That's the left side of the ship. Since we know he was in the North Atlantic from his last letter, then the land he saw had to be Europe. And if Europe was on his left, then the ship was headed south. So the blacked-out word is 'south.' Pops is headed south."

"I always knew I had a genius for a son." Mom took off her hat and shook out her hair. "Did you take the cookies to the Twekenberrys?"

"You're not going to believe this, Mom, but while I was there a telegram came. They found Jim and he's alive."

Mom put her hand on her heart and tears sprang to her eyes. "Oh, Francis, it's a miracle. Truly it is. To think a young man has been snatched from the jaws of death. They must be overjoyed."

"I'll say they are. The Twekenberrys sure know how to celebrate. Rosemarie's aunts and uncles were shouting and hugging and dancing. You should have seen them. And Mrs. Twekenberry turned out to be real nice."

Mom looked so happy. I hated to tell her the rest. "The news wasn't all good, Mom. Jim was wounded, and they're shipping him to a hospital somewhere in Florida."

Mom's face puckered with worry as she lit a fire under the tea kettle. "Now that's a shame. How serious is it?"

"No one knows," I answered, "but they're all praying for him."

Mom patted me on the back. "The Navy will take good care of him. At least he's alive and coming home."

"Hey, that's exactly what Mr. Twekenberry said."

Mom poured herself a cup of tea and settled down with the Sunday paper. I got out my algebra book and started on my homework.

I was still working on the first problem when Mom started in. "'Big Three Leaders Believed on Way Home from Teheran Conference,'" she read. Here we go, I thought. Mom can't read to herself no matter what. And that was only the headlines. "'President Roosevelt, Prime Minister Churchill, and Premier Stalin,'" Mom continued, "'withheld official word on plans for a Second Front offensive. But hopes run high.'"

Mom lowered the paper. "Do you have any idea what this means, Francis? If Russia attacks Germany on the east, the

Nazis will have to fight on both their eastern and western boundaries. That will be their undoing. They'll have to surrender." Mom banged her hand on the table. "The sooner, the better! I want Pops home."

"Boy, me too, Mom," I said. I went back to my homework.

Seconds later I heard, "Tsk, tsk, tsk." I looked up. Mom was shaking her head.

" 'Atlantic City Fire Causes Five Hundred Thousand Dollar Loss.' Now, isn't that a pity?"

"Sure is," I said, wishing Mom would read to herself.

Three more problems solved, then "Mmm. Mmm! The temperature's rising to eighty-one degrees today. Eighty-one in December. Imagine that. Philadelphia's high is only going to be in the fifties. I do like this warm Florida weather."

"Mom, you're not helping. How do you expect me to get my homework done if you keep reading everything out loud?"

Mom gave a little sigh, but she stopped. Thinking about how she and Pops always shared the Sunday paper, ads and all, I felt kind of bad I'd said anything. I guess she was really missing Pops.

With Mom quiet, I whizzed through a dozen problems and neared the end when I heard Mom sip air. Looking up, I saw her hand fly to her mouth.

"What?" I asked.

She looked at my open book and waved her hand in the air and shook her head.

"It's okay, Mom, I'm through."

She eyed me doubtfully, but I know Mom, she couldn't hold back. "The Jacksonville police had their hands full last night. It says right here, and I quote, 'Shortly after midnight a Mr. Dean Adams tried to open his rented storage locker at the train station. He expressed frustration that his key didn't work. Not realizing he had the wrong locker, he forced the lock.'"

Mom looked up and gave me her you'll-never-guess look. "What do you think they found inside?"

"A baby?" I shot back.

Mom rolled her eyes. "Be serious, Francis. Mr. Adams found a package that made a strange ticking sound."

I raised an eyebrow. "A clock?"

Mom's lips thinned into a straight line. She didn't appreciate my conclusions. "The package held a time bomb."

"Wow!" I popped my gum. "Did the bomb go off?"

"Fortunately not," Mom answered. "The police defused it in time. It was set to explode at nine this morning when the terminal would have been filled with servicemen and their families seeing them off." Mom slumped back in her chair and shook her head slowly back and forth. "What monster would do such a horrible thing? Right here in Jacksonville. Who could imagine?"

And that's when my imagination kicked in. A bomb. A spy. A spy and a bomb. A spy turned saboteur. Who else could it be? I cracked my knuckles hard. "Mom, did they catch the person who planted the bomb?"

Mom ran her finger on down the column. "Yes, indeed. The police arrested a Joseph Hawkins. He was fired a week ago as station master and had written several letters to the railroad company threatening revenge."

I sat there drumming my fingers on the table. "I don't think they got the right man. Planting a bomb sounds to me more like something a spy would do."

"Not that spy nonsense again, Francis?"

"Well, the bomb was set to go off when the station was

full of servicemen. That's the kind of thing a spy does."

Mom got out her nail file. She pressed her lips in a straight line and began to file like mad. "They've already arrested a man, Francis."

I could see I was getting nowhere. I reached for my history book and opened it to chapter seven. I stared at the page, thinking. Something gnawed at my brain, but I didn't know what. "I'm going down to the beach for a while, okay, Mom?"

I hadn't taken ten steps out the door when it struck me. 5-12-43. The second date on the paper! Today! The same day as the bomb was set to go off. If I had any doubts before, that convinced me. It had to be the spy who planted that bomb! I don't know anything about disgruntled railroad workers, but I know that worker didn't plant any bomb unless he was in cahoots with the spy. Code busted or not, the police needed to know, and they needed to know before December seventh, the next date on the paper. Who knew what catastrophe the spy planned for that day?

Ten minutes later, I was banging on Wanda's door. Was she ever surprised to see me! I'd been there less than two hours before to tell her about Rosemarie's brother. This time, I went in talking. "Listen, Wanda, you gotta go to the police with me. I need you there. I'm even thinking about skipping school. Well, I can't do that. There's too much at stake there too. But the minute school's out, I'm heading to the police station. If Rosemarie thinks her music lesson is so all-fired important, then she'll just have to miss out. Did you read in the paper about the bomb at the train station?"

Boy, I couldn't stop talking. I paced back and forth as I explained about the dates. How the first date on the paper matched up with the day the spy landed, and the second matched up with the bomb at the train station. "I'm convinced something terrible will happen on the third date. That's the seventh of December, Pearl Harbor Day, the same day Japan forced us into this war by bombing Hawaii."

Wanda understood all right, but she was as stubborn as before. "But why, Wanda?" I pleaded. "Why won't you go?"

Wanda's eyelashes fluttered. She straightened her back. "I... I... I don't like people making fun of me."

"If you'd ditch those army boots and that ratty trench coat and dress like a normal person, they wouldn't make fun of you."

Wanda's blue eye, and her brown eye too, glared at me. "In... In... In case you've forgotten, I... I... I stutter. B... B... Bad."

I couldn't think of anything to say. She was right. She did stutter something awful. Then I remembered something from yesterday when we worked on making the spy's message visible. "Do you have any matches?" I asked.

Wanda gave me a curious look but brought me a box of kitchen matches. I picked up a piece of loose-leaf paper and headed for the kitchen. Holding the paper over a plate, I struck a match and touched the edge of the paper. It burst into flame. Wanda dashed over. She blew hard and put out the fire. She turned on me, her eyes flashing. "Are you crazy? Do you want to burn down the house?"

I crossed my arms and grinned. "Just as I thought. No stutter."

Wanda blinked her eyes. "I... I... I don't understand."

"Yesterday after you blew out the candle, you didn't stutter. And today after blowing out the fire, you didn't stutter. Don't you see? Whenever you blow, you don't stutter. Try it."

Wanda pursed her lips and blew. Puff... like she was

blowing away a pesky bug.

I smacked my forehead. "For crying out loud, blow like you mean it. Pretend you have to blow out eighteen candles on a birthday cake."

Wanda nodded and blew hard. Then she stood there, looking panic-stricken. I nodded encouragement.

"M... M... M..." Her shoulders sagged.

"You waited too long. Come on, Wanda, try again. I know it will work. Take a deep breath and blow hard. You have to start talking right away."

Wanda rolled her eyes, but she blew hard and started talking. "My name is Wanda Barr."

"Hooray! You did it."

Wanda's face lit up like a full moon. She grinned real big. No more twitchy lips. It was the first time I saw her smile like she really meant it. I realized Wanda was, well, pretty. Not just kind of pretty, but a real knockout. Her teeth flashed white and straight, dimples appeared in her cheeks, and her eyes danced like fireflies. Wow. Wanda flicked her long hair behind her ears. She blew again. "Frank, you're one smart fella. Thanks."

"You're welcome," I said, running water over the cooled ashes. "So we're all set for tomorrow?"

Wanda giggled.

"What's so funny?" I asked. Her giggle turned to laughing. She dropped into a chair. Tears ran down her cheeks as she tried to stop. Gasping for breath, she blew a mighty blow.

"If I huff and puff every time I speak,"—she blew again—"people will think I'm crazier than they already do."

Wanda released another deep breath. "Here's something even stranger. I don't stutter when I sing, either." And darned if Wanda didn't burst into song. She created new lyrics to the tune of "There's a Tavern in the Town" and sang:

"There's a spy near my house, near my house.

And he's sneaky as a mouse, as a mouse."

Now it was my turn to burst out laughing. "That would sure get the police's attention."

"A... A... And they'd laugh at me too and th... th... think it was all a joke."

"Then don't sing. Just blow. I need you to back me up and tell about the cigarettes and how you knew the formula that brought out the coded message. If there's two of us, there's a better chance they'll believe us. You've got to come. Please?"

"Y... Y... You don't need me."

I snapped my gum hard, completely frustrated by Wanda's stubbornness. "Look Wanda, I'm going to the police as soon as school's out at three fifteen. Which means I'll be there by three twenty. I really need your support."

I backed out the door. "I'm counting on you. Don't let me down." Trying to look as stern as Pops when he gave me lectures, I measured out my final words. "See... you... there."

14

Crazy Monday

Monday morning, Mr. Jolly was in a frenzy. He pranced from one side of the room to the other, waving his arms. "Changed the date of the rally!" Slam! Bang! He pounded his fist on the desk.

"One day to prepare!" Slam! Bang! On the windowsill.

"Stuck in our classroom!" Slam! Bang! On Rosemarie's desk. She shrank back, blinking up at him.

Mr. Jolly stopped. He looked down at Rosemarie. He lowered his voice and grew grave. "I was sorry to hear that Jim was wounded, Rosemarie. Your brother is a fine young man."

"He's coming home, Mr. Jolly. He'll be all right. I know he will."

"Good, good," Mr. Jolly murmured. He patted Rosemarie on the shoulder. Maybe the thought of a former student wounded in the jungles of the South Pacific made Mr. Jolly realize that his problem, whatever it was, wasn't so important. He paced silently. We all watched as he moved back and forth, deep in thought, his hands behind his back, strands of hair dangling over his eyebrows.

Suddenly, in one quick movement, he raised an arm high. "Laaaadies and gentlemen and alllll my distinguished students, we have a problem. The date of the war bond rally at St. Johns

River Shipyard has been changed. It will take place tomorrow, December seventh."

I felt the color drain right out of me. 7-12-43. Mom's shipyard! The seventh was the next date on the spy's list. The shipyard was the perfect place to plant a bomb or set a fire or do something too horrible to imagine. My throat started to close up.

I forgot where I was and snapped my gum. Mr. Jolly glared. That was enough to snap me out of my panic. I removed my gum and tried to think logically. Number one: The spy would already have his target lined up. Number two: He'd never hear about the change of dates. Yeah, we'd be safe enough at the shipyard. Nothing to worry about there. I shifted in my seat. But the spy was going to strike somewhere. If only we had broken the code. If only it were three fifteen and I could get to the police. I'd be glad to turn the whole mess over to them.

Mr. Jolly kept talking. I tried to listen, but my mind whirled.

"We must complete all preparations for the bond rally today. Today, I say!" Mr. Jolly pounded his fist into his hand like a dot on an exclamation point. "We are hampered by lack of space to prepare for tomorrow's bond rally, because the gym is off-limits for the entire day."

Mr. Jolly's face grew red. "Whose bumbling idea was it to put Spanish moss in the gym? Chiggers! That's what you brought. Chiggers! A parasite of the family *Trombiculidae*. They bite. They itch. They cancel dances. Are you aware those pesky bugs caused your Sadie Hawkins Day dance to be canceled? These chiggers must be destroyed. That is why at this very moment the exterminators are fumigating the gym. And that is why we have no place to complete our preparations."

Mr. Jolly narrowed his eyes. "Those of you who are responsible for this debacle know who you are." He leaned toward us and arched a brow.

I glanced around the room. Howard stared out the window. Lloyd gazed up at the ceiling, following the slow progress of a fly that had stopped to preen its wings. Joey shuffled his feet. Even Gladys acted peculiar—well, peculiar for Gladys. She sat with her hands folded and her mouth shut.

I leaned toward Joey. "Is he saying there wasn't any dance?"

Joey held out his arm. It was covered with red welts. Guess that answered my question.

Mr. Jolly jerked back his head. His gaze swept the room. Then he took a deep breath and exhaled like a deflated balloon.

"In time of war we must move forward. With haste. We will," he said, bracing himself, "forget the gym. We will make final preparations in this, our classroom." Mr. Jolly heaved a great shudder.

We all watched in fascination as he quivered from jowls to belly to knees. The fight went out of him, but only for a minute. He straightened his shoulders and issued his command. "Move forward with haste, I say."

Mr. Jolly's words spoke to me, but not about the rally. I wanted to make haste all right, haste to the police. But here I was stuck in the classroom until three fifteen. My stomach churned. *Okay, Frank Hollahan, calm down,* I told myself. *Get through the school day, then to the police. They'll listen. They've got to listen. It's going to be okay.* I closed down any thoughts of the spy and concentrated on Mr. Jolly.

"Those who were assigned posters—that means every-one—show me your wares."

Uh-oh! That was the one assignment I didn't get around to over the weekend. I hoped Mr. Jolly wouldn't notice.

Gladys, of course, was the first to pop up from her seat. Lloyd was right behind her. I noticed most of the slogans were borrowed from posters that already hung across the United States. BUY A BOND TODAY—BONDS FOR FREEDOM—BUY BONDS AND BRING OUR BOYS HOME—HAVE YOU BOUGHT YOUR BOND TODAY? I wished I'd thought of doing that. But I never could have come up with such swell pictures.

Howard's sign listed the price of the war bonds. Eighteen dollars and seventy-five cents for a bond that would pay back twenty-five dollars in ten years. Thirty-seven dollars and fifty cents for a fifty-dollar bond and seventy-five dollars for a hundred-dollar bond. All the bond money went toward building battleships, war planes, tanks, and whatever else we needed to win the war.

I had already bought two bonds in bits and pieces. I'd bought one twenty-five-cent war stamp at a time until I had enough for each of the twenty-five-dollar bonds. Right now, a half-filled book of pasted-in stamps sat on my bookcase at home.

Rosemarie made two special signs for people like me: STAMPS STAMP OUT THE ENEMY and A STAMP A DAY KEEPS THE ENEMY AWAY.

Even though they had nothing to do with buying bonds, some of the guys made other patriotic signs like they'd seen around town. SHH! LOOSE LIPS SINK SHIPS and SAVE YOUR TIN CANS were the favorites. Joey drew a picture of Uncle Sam, saying I WANT YOU. When I looked at that poster, I got the feeling Uncle Sam was pointing right at me. I'll bet, after seeing Joey's poster, some of the men at the rally will join the service.

I was busy admiring Joey's poster when a shadow crossed my desk. I shifted my eyes to the right. Mr. Jolly stood over me. "And where is your poster, Mr. Hollahan?"

I cleared my throat. I wasn't sure what I was going to say, but I knew it had better be good. "Well, it's like this, Mr. Jolly," I began. "My lack of accomplishment is due entirely to mitigating circumstances. I was about to proceed with my assignment when I was interrupted by certain members of this class, who arranged to rendezvous in my front yard. Naturally, I felt obliged to assist in their endeavor."

I was tossing out some of my best vocabulary, but Mr. Jolly didn't look impressed. He eyed me suspiciously as I plodded on. I told him of my magnificent rescue of Juniper, of my visit to Rosemarie's, and of the wonder of the telegram. I was careful to conceal any of my activities concerning the spy. What I had was too good for Mr. Jolly. It was definitely worthy of the police and the police only.

I finally ended with, "And it was only due to pure exhaustion that I failed to undertake the assignment." I was quick to add, "But I will get to it immediately."

"My, my, my," Mr. Jolly said. "You do have a gift for the gab. Since you have such a wonderful way with words, Frank, you may prepare a rousing speech as to why people should buy bonds. To be delivered at the rally." I groaned. "You may spend the day in preparation."

School dragged on forever. While the girls practiced for leading the crowd in singing patriotic songs, I jotted down my first inspiration. While the guys stepped outside and practiced marching, I slaved over my speech. Now and then, my mind wandered to the police station. While the girls made paper costumes from red, white, and blue crepe paper, Mr. Jolly stood over me. Quickly, I managed another thought and got down a few more lines.

Time dragged. Here I was, working on a speech I didn't want to give. What I needed was time to think about how I could best present my evidence to the police. The coded paper in my pocket felt hot on my leg. I kept checking to make sure it was there. And Mr. Jolly kept checking on me. Two minutes before dismissal, he finally approved what I'd written. The second the final bell rang, I was out the door like a war hawk.

15

Precinct #49

I ran like crazy down Eighth Avenue. When I reached First Street, I swung right and flew past Dickerson's Hardware and Beach Jewelry, nearly running down an old lady leaving Ye Little Dress Shoppe. When the Beach Theater came into view, I knew I was almost there. I dashed under the movie marquee advertising *Beyond the Blue Horizon*, starring the hubba-hubba pin-up, Dorothy Lamour. I turned left and skidded to a halt two inches short of Wanda. "Boy, am I glad to see you," I said.

Wanda pursed her lips and blew to stop her stuttering. She rolled her brown eye and maybe her blue. "I'm here," she said.

I held open the door to the police station. "Stay calm. Follow my lead."

Square in the center of the nearly barren room was a huge desk. Behind the desk sat a big, burly cop with his cap pushed back on his head. His nameplate told me he was Sergeant Higgins. Wanted posters of some mean-looking characters hung on dingy walls. Keys that probably belonged to the jail cells down a long hall to the right dangled from a key ring on a peg. Maybe the poor guy wrongly accused of planting the bomb was withering away in one of the cells.

Sergeant Higgins looked Wanda and me over pretty good.

"What can I do for you?" he asked gruffly.

Perspiration beaded on my forehead. Pops always said the police were our friends, but this guy made me nervous. "Eh, uh, I want to report a sighting of a submarine. Not just any sub, but a Nazi U-boat. It was last Wednesday night. The first of December, to be exact."

Sergeant Higgins gave me an odd look but then just pushed his cap farther back on his head and leaned forward. "Go on."

"I saw a man come ashore. He came from the sub."

"Did you actually see this man leave this U-boat you claim you saw?"

"Not exactly. But he came walking right out of the ocean. And he was carrying a chest of some sort. He buried it in the sand and left."

The cop squinted up his right eye and raised his left brow. "Sounds like a bad dream to me. Sure you didn't dream it?"

"No, sir, I saw him with my own eyes."

Sergeant Higgins pulled a tablet toward him and picked up a pencil. "Give me a description of the man."

"Well, it was awfully dark. I couldn't really tell much, except that he was tall."

"Tall as your friend here?" He jerked his thumb toward Wanda, then asked her, "Did you see this man come out of the sea?"

Wanda blew. "No, sir."

The cop gave her a funny look. "Is this your sister, kid?"

Wanda blew again. "I'm his neighbor." I could tell she was feeling good about getting out two whole sentences without a stutter.

Then the sarge ruined it all. He stood up and crossed his beefy arms across his chest. "What's all this huffing and puffing? You the big bad wolf?" He threw his head back and laughed at his own dumb joke.

Wanda got red in the face, and her eyelashes went into a fast flutter.

"It's okay," I said. I turned back to the sergeant. "Look, that guy I saw is a spy. We found a coded message and another paper with dates, and we saw signs that somebody was holing up in the cabanas on the beach. I'd be willing to bet he's the guy who planted the bomb at the train station. And..."

"Hold it, sonny." The sergeant stuck his head in the door behind him. "Hey, Chief, there's some kid out here spreading dangerous rumors. Says he saw a German spy dropped off by a U-boat."

A second later, a short, skinny guy, who looked like anyone but a police chief, stepped into the room. He planted his feet far apart and hooked his thumbs in his belt. He cocked his head and eyed me like he was inspecting something bad. "You in Mr. Jolly's class at the junior high?"

I nodded. How the heck did he know that?

"So you're the kid I've been hearing about?"

I glanced at Wanda. She looked as puzzled as I was. "From who... I mean, from whom?" I asked.

"My daughter's in your class. My Gladys is a fountain of information."

I double-popped my knuckles. What lousy luck. Why did the chief have to be Gladys' dad?

"The kid's got a good imagination," the sergeant said. He turned to me. "You got a good imagination, kid."

I pulled myself up to my full height. "Look, sir. Between Wanda and me and her dog, Juniper, we found some good evidence." I reached into my pocket and whipped out the coded paper and packet. "Wanda's dog found this buried in the sand, wrapped in this oilcloth cover. It was near where the chest was buried."

"Ah, the disappearing chest," said Chief Flagg, reaching for the paper. "Did you ever find that chest?"

"No, sir. I think the spy came back and retrieved it before I had a chance to find it."

"Hmm," he mumbled as he studied the paper.

"That paper was blank when we found it, but Wanda knew how to bring out the message. Right, Wanda?"

Wanda nodded, and I realized the sergeant's remarks had ended any blowing or smooth talking.

"There was an empty pack of German cigarettes," I said, "but Wanda accidentally burned that in her fireplace. And another paper was destroyed too. I guess Gladys told you about that. It had dates on it. I remember the first three. I think they're all important."

The chief handed me back the paper. "Looks to me like you printed these yourself. Did you do the same with the dates?"

Boy, that made me crazy. Wanda too, I guess. We both started talking at the same time, our words tumbling over one another. "You've got to believe me!"

"F... F... Frank's telling the t... t... truth."

"Look how they make the sevens."

"T... T... The German way. A... A... And I saw the p... p... pack of cigarettes. C... C... Cigarettes spelled with a z."

"The dates are important. He landed on the first, the bomb went off on the fifth. Tomorrow's the seventh. I tell you, something bad is going to happen."

"S... S... Something b... b... bad."

Wanda's stutter, the worst I ever heard, seemed to amuse the sergeant. He nudged the chief, pointed his thumb at

Wanda, and snickered. The chief cut his laugh short with a sharp glance. Maybe he wasn't such a bad guy after all. But Wanda had heard the snicker and closed down completely. I couldn't even make eye contact with her.

Finally, Chief Flagg held up his hand. "Look, Frank, I don't know what you're trying to pull here. Some new kid looking for attention, wanting to be noticed, is that it? Well, let me tell you, you've been noticed all right. And it's not good. We've listened to you and seen your evidence. Honestly, I'm not impressed."

He reached out and took Wanda's elbow in a fatherly gesture. "I don't know how Frank convinced you to get involved, Wanda. I thought you were smarter than that. Guess having your brother overseas and your living alone makes you a little edgy. Trust me. You're as safe as my Gladys."

I balled up my fists in frustration. "That's what I'm trying to tell you, Chief. Gladys isn't safe. None of us is safe as long as that spy's loose. You've got to do something."

The chief held onto Wanda's arm and grabbed mine, none too gently, and propelled us out the door. "If I hear any more about a spy, I promise you that the consequences will be very serious."

I jammed my fists into my pockets and kicked the curb. Rosemarie came dashing around the corner. "My music teacher canceled. I got here as soon as I could. Did you talk to the police already? How did it go?"

Wanda blew. "Not well," she said. Boy, was that ever the understatement of the year.

We headed for Lee's Drugstore, and I explained everything to Rosemarie on the way. "I thought for sure we had enough to convince them," I said as we slid into a booth. "But they hardly listened. They didn't believe anything.

They thought our clues were fakes. We're definitely on our own."

Rosemarie just shook her head, and the three of us fell silent. As we sipped our sodas, I reviewed what we knew. "Here's what we've got." I counted on my fingers. "One: We know when something's likely to happen—on the seventh of December. Two: We know what's likely to happen—something will get blown up. The big question is: Where? There's got to be a way to figure this out and stop the spy. And we'd better think of something fast."

16

The Missing Piece

E arly on the morning of the seventh, with the sun barely up, I pulled on my school clothes and slipped out the door. I was so riled up over the spy, I couldn't concentrate on my speech. I headed for the beach, hoping the salt air would clear my head and calm the knots in my stomach.

"Remember Pearl Harbor!" I shouted as I crossed the dunes. I thrust my right arm forward in a magnificent sweep. That should get the crowd's attention. "Two years ago our enemy bombed Pearl Harbor. Thousands of lives were lost, our mighty ships destroyed. You here at the shipyard have contributed to the rebuilding of our navy, making it once again the mightiest in the world. But there is still more that you can do for our men and women overseas, more that you can do to keep the enemy from our shores."

Those words brought me to a standstill. We hadn't kept our enemy from our shores. Boy, here was my chance to tell what I knew. But would they believe me? I was deep in thought when I started up the last dune. A flash of light coming off the water startled me. I crouched down and ducked behind a clump of palmettos. The hair rose on the back of my neck. Standing practically on the spot where I'd first seen the spy was a rugged-looking man with blond hair whipped by the wind.

The man held a small shiny object in his hand that he tipped back and forth. The sun bounced off its surface, sometimes short flashes, sometimes long, like Morse code. It was Morse code! Offshore came flickers of light in dots and dashes. I made out a periscope, the spyglass of a submarine.

Holy cow! The spy!

At last I was seeing the spy. Maybe he was signaling the submarine to pick him up. Maybe he would leave as mysteriously as he had appeared, but with a bomb already planted.

My heart pounded in my ears. My chest felt like it would explode. More dots and dashes. Pops had tried to teach me Morse code. He told me it would come in handy some day—but who would have guessed that today would be the day? I flipped my speech paper over to the blank side and whipped out my pencil. Blunt as a hammerhead, but it would have to do. Who knew how long they'd been flashing? I picked up what I could.

If I were Superman, I'd snatch that spy up by the collar and haul him to the police. Wouldn't they be surprised to hear German rolling off his tongue? Or, if I were Mandrake the Magician, I'd shrink him to the size of my thumb, stick him in my pocket, and deliver him to Gladys' dad at the police station. Gee whiz, I was thinking like a little kid. Maybe I should rush him and throw him to the ground. But then what? Besides, he made nearly two of me.

The spy turned toward the dunes and started walking. Toward me! Right then I'd have liked to have been one of those land crabs that always scurried across the sand and disappeared down a hole. I didn't dare breathe. I prayed my shoes weren't sticking out from my hiding place.

Halfway to the dunes, the spy stopped and lit a cigarette. He was close enough that I could see his nicotine-stained fingers and perfectly manicured nails, even neater than Mom's. He crumpled the empty pack. It was the same color as the piece I'd found in Wanda's fireplace. He heaved the aquamarine wad into the surf. I watched, helpless, as it rode out to sea on the waves.

If luck would get me through this without the spy seeing me, I could get a good description. I studied his firm jaw, square face, and skinny yellow mustache. He had a mole on his neck that was half hidden by his upturned collar. He wore tan pants and a gray jacket.

He began walking, not toward the cabanas, but in the opposite direction. I sprinted to the next bunch of palmettos, planning to follow him, but he jogged along the shore at a fast pace, checking over his shoulder every few seconds, then turned inland and disappeared out of sight.

I took off like sixty. In the other direction. I ran toward Wanda's, stumbling and falling more times than I'd ever admit.

"Open up! Open up!" I shouted as I pounded on her door. I danced from foot to foot. Finally, Wanda, wrapped in a blanket, opened the door a crack and peered out. Never mind the niceties. I pushed past her. "I saw him, Wanda. He was *this* close." I held my fingers apart like I was measuring a minnow. Wanda stared at me like I was a wild man. I guess I was a little crazy.

Wanda took a deep breath and blew. "Who did you see?"

That stopped me cold. I stared back, then put my face close to hers, which wasn't very close, more like I was talking to her neck. "The spy!" I said through clenched teeth. I stepped back to see if my words registered.

Wanda nodded.

"He used a mirror to communicate with a U-boat by

Morse code. I got there at the end so I didn't get much down. Just this." I held up my jottings for Wanda to see. "It's hard to tell where one letter ends and another begins, but I think I got it. Dot-dot-dot. That's *s*. Dash-dot-dash-dot. That's *c*. Dot-dot-dot-dot. *h*. Let's see, that's *sch*. Gee willikers, the spy's going to blow up a school!"

"K… K… Keep going," Wanda said. She leaned over my shoulder, crowding me, making me a wreck.

I got stuck on the next letter, but Wanda knew it. We worked through the rest in no time flat. Wanda remembered to blow. "So what do we have?" she asked.

I stared at the letters: "schiffbau," I read. "Well, I can tell you one thing. It sure isn't school. It's nothing." I slouched back in the chair and popped my knuckles one at a time.

Wanda continued to stare at the word. She frowned. "I… I… I think that's a German word."

"Huh?" I mumbled, scratching my head. Wanda disappeared and came back with a German-English Dictionary. I began to think her library was better than the public one.

"Here it is," Wanda said. She thrust the book at me and pointed to—I couldn't believe my eyes—*schiffbau*. As I read the definition, my heart beat fast, then faster.

I jumped up from the table. "Shipbuilding! Do you know what this means, Wanda? The shipyard! The perfect place for a disaster. A bomb going off there would wreck morale, not to mention what it would do to the people and the ships. Did you know the bond rally at the shipyard was changed to today?"

Wanda nodded and blew. "I heard it on the radio."

I cracked my knuckles. "I'll bet the spy did too. He'd never be able to get in there on a normal day when they check identifications. But they're not checking today. The whole city is invited. The gates will be wide open. He'll slip in easy as sliding on a slick of oil."

Wanda blew extra hard. "We need to go back to the police."

"You've got to be kidding, Wanda. They didn't believe anything we told them yesterday. We've got to stop this guy on our own." I grabbed a magazine from the coffee table and fished the pencil out of my pocket. "Like I said, the last I saw of the spy, he turned up the path toward the main road." I sketched the beach, path, and the highway. "I'll bet you my entire collection of Indian-head nickels that he's headed for town and the rally." I drew an arrow pointing toward Jacksonville.

"Wanda, you've got to come to the bond rally and help me spot him. Finding the spy in the crowd is our only hope. I'll be on the stage and I'll be watching, but you'll have a better chance being in the crowd. When you spot him…"

"If… If… If I spot him."

"*When* you spot him," I said, emphasizing the "when," "give me a signal. I'll be watching from the stage."

"Th… Th… Then what?"

"I don't know. I'll figure something out. Just remember what he looks like. He's nearly as tall as you are. He's blond. His fingers are stained from nicotine. He's wearing a gray zippered jacket and dark tan pants. But most of all, look for a small blond mustache and the mole on his neck. That should clear up any doubts."

Wanda blew. "What if he's wearing a hat?

"A hat won't cover the mole."

Blow, blow. "What if he turns up his collar?"

"I don't know, Wanda." Why did she have to make everything so hard? "Just do it, will you?"

I turned to leave then swung back around. "Maybe you're right about the police, Wanda. But I don't have time before school. It's up to you. Swing by on your way to the rally and I'll alert Mr. Jolly. The more people working on this, the better."

17

Rally 'Round the Flag

I dashed into class at the last second. Mr. Jolly looked like a trapeze artist, flying from one side of the room to the other with last-minute instructions for everyone. While he was helping Gladys reshape her Statue of Liberty torch, which looked more like the Leaning Tower of Pisa, I pulled Rosemarie aside. "I saw him, Rosemarie."

"Who?"

"The spy! I saw the spy."

Rosemarie's eyes grew big. "No kidding? What did he look like?"

"Big, blond, and brawny." And I told her everything.

"Golly," she said. "This is getting scary."

"Yeah, but I have a plan. Wanda's going to weave in and out of the crowd and signal me when she sees him."

"Then what?" Rosemarie asked.

"Girls," I snarled. "Always wanting the last detail."

"Well?"

"I haven't decided. It depends," I muttered as I moved away, rustling the pages of my speech. I'd racked my brain all morning for an idea and had come up empty. It was churning my stomach to mush. I wish I knew if Wanda made it to the police or lost her nerve. I wanted to warn Mr. Jolly, but he kept on the move, issuing orders like a drill sergeant. By the time my class boarded the bus for downtown Jacksonville and St. Johns Shipyard, we all knew exactly what we should do. The rally was due to begin at twelve o'clock sharp. I was still trying to get Mr. Jolly's attention when we rolled up to the shipyard gate at ten minutes before noon.

I peered out the window. What a mob! Crowds streamed down the sidewalks, spilled across the street, and swarmed through the gate. I didn't know there were that many people in Jacksonville. Inside the shipyard, workers in coveralls and denim caps had already gathered in little groups waiting for the rally to begin. I scanned the crowds but couldn't spot Wanda or the spy. There wasn't a policeman in sight.

As we stood in the aisle waiting to get off the bus, I whispered to Rosemarie, "I decided on a plan. When Wanda signals, I'm going to grab the mike and tell the world." But Rosemarie had the jitters so bad over her singing role, she only stared at me like I was a total stranger.

Gladys, dressed like the Statue of Liberty, her torch repaired, led the way. The other girls wore nifty red, white, and blue crepe-paper skirts and hats. They charged off the bus right behind Gladys, looking like a giant U.S. flag unfurling. Holding their posters high, they cheered and danced their way through the crowd towards the stage. People made way and applauded as they passed. The guys followed. Everyone marched in perfect formation. Except me. Not having practiced, I couldn't stop my left foot from tangling with my right. I was a step behind or a bounce to the side during the entire march.

We filed up the steps and onto the stage. Roger placed the flag in its stand and stepped back to lead the Pledge of Allegiance. Everyone saluted or held his hand over his heart, his eyes fixed on the stars and stripes. It made me proud to be an American. After the pledge, Rosemarie's high, clear voice sang the first notes of the "Star Spangled Banner." More than a thousand voices joined in singing the National Anthem. It was enough to give a guy goose bumps.

Finally I spotted Wanda's head bobbing above everyone else's as she moved through the crowd. Super tall was cool. I couldn't see my pal Juniper but knew he was prancing along beside her in case of trouble.

The cheerleaders led the crowd in patriotic cheers, then settled behind me on the stage floor. That was my cue. My hands sweat like crazy as I took my place at the microphone and looked out over the crowd. A zillion people stood in the sun or slumped against a wall seeking shade and waited to hear me—me!—Frank Hollahan—deliver a speech telling them to buy bonds.

I placed my right hand on my breast and made a sweeping gesture with my left, Mr. Jolly-style. I turned to my left to get Mr. Jolly's reaction to my excellent imitation of him. He sat with his back straight as starch, his arms extended, hands resting on his knees, and his ample belly bulging over his notched leather belt. He smiled and nodded his approval.

I cleared my throat and began. "Remember Pearl Harbor!" My voice resounded through the mike and echoed off the factory walls. Howard, sitting directly in front of the stage, looked up at me and rolled his eyes. He put a finger in one ear, the one on the side away from Mr. Jolly. Lloyd picked up on Howard's move and made a face like he'd tasted something sour. Let them have their fun. I had an important speech to deliver, and I wasn't going to let them throw me off.

"Ladies and gentlemen and alllll the patriotic citizens of Jacksonville," I said, ignoring the guys and playing to the crowd, who waited in quiet anticipation. "Two years ago, our enemy bombed Pearl Harbor. Thousands of lives were lost, our mighty ships destroyed. You, here at the shipyard, have contributed to the rebuilding of our navy." I was on a roll, riveting the audience. I forgot about the spy, forgot about Rosemarie, forgot about Wanda, who at this very moment was tracking down the most dangerous man in Jacksonville.

I was spectacular, magnificent. I had the crowd in the palm of my hand. The girls behind shouted "Rah! Rah! Rah!" I glanced back. Rosemarie smiled. Her butterscotch eyes sparkled in the sun. My voice rose, challenging the crowd. "Lift our country from the clutches of the enemy. Buy a bond today."

I was about to present my most compelling argument for them to part with their money when I felt a tug like a cat's claw just below my knee on the back of my pants leg. I shook my leg. Another tug. I swatted the back of my knee, never missing a beat in my speech. Then came a yank. A strong one. So strong that I had to hike up my pants so I wouldn't lose them. I looked back.

"Wanda's signaling," Rosemarie hissed.

Confused, I mumbled a few more words of my speech. I looked for Wanda over the heads of the milling crowd but couldn't find her. Then I heard singing. Far away singing. One lonely voice. "All hail to the red, white, and blue." It sounded like Wanda. But no stuttering. Then I remembered: she doesn't stutter when she sings.

I stopped talking. A few people joined in the next line of the song. "All hail to the red, white, and blue." The singing grew louder. "May our banner of freedom reign forever." It ended with wild enthusiasm. "All hail to the red, white, and blue."

My eyes scanned the crowd as people broke into a patriotic cheer. I spotted Wanda off to one side. She had a finger partially hidden behind her hand, pointing to her right. I caught a glimpse of a man in a cap and jacket the color of the spy's. And I'm pretty sure I detected his skinny pencil mustache.

"Get that man," I cried, pointing. "He's a spy."

The man didn't move. Neither did anyone else. Someone laughed. Laughed like he thought it was a joke, a part of the speech. Others joined in the laughter.

Oh, boy, had I misread Wanda's signal? But no, she'd stepped back from the man. She kept bobbing her head and mouthing the word "spy."

"That's him!" I cried. "The man in the blue cap. He's a spy. A saboteur! A bomber! Over there by Wanda. The tall girl. Wave your arms, Wanda."

Wanda waved her arms, and people laughed all the louder. The spy wasn't moving, but he wasn't laughing, either.

I glanced at Mom, who had been standing so proud just a minute ago. Now her face registered disbelief. She crossed her arms and pressed her lips into a straight line. I could read her mind—*Not the spy. Again!*

A man shouted, "Get the kid off the stage!"

From the corner of my eye, I saw a red-faced Mr. Jolly rise from his seat and stomp towards me.

"Let's hear the boy out," someone called.

Rosemarie cupped her hands around her mouth. "Frank, the spy's moving."

"There he goes," I yelled. I watched the spy work his way through the crowd toward one of the buildings. "Stop him. He's a spy. Honest!" No one even seemed to notice him. Mr.

Jolly wrapped his beefy hand around my arm. I pulled away and tried to jump off the stage. I had to stop the spy. But Mr. Jolly's grip was too strong. "I saw a Nazi U-boat drop that man off on the beach," I cried. "He lost this paper," I said, pulling it from my pocket. "It has a hidden message." I waved the paper at the crowd as Mr. Jolly jerked me away from the mike.

Rosemarie jumped up and took my place. "It's true!" she shouted into the mike. "Everything Frank is telling you is true. Something terrible is scheduled to happen today."

People stopped laughing. They turned to one another. They began whispering. The spy, with Wanda in pursuit, had nearly reached the building with the big smokestacks.

"Stop the spy!" I shouted again. This time people turned, trying to see where I pointed. "Don't let him get away!" I hollered. Mr. Jolly dragged me down the platform steps. A hand gripped my other arm. I looked up. A man in a coat and tie tipped his hat and flashed a badge.

Mr. Jolly released his grip. "Looks like you're in real trouble now, Hollahan," he said. Another man took Mr. Jolly's place. Both men flashed their badges again. This time in my face. FBI!

The first man leaned toward me. "The Beach Police contacted us. Said we'd find you here. We need to have a little talk, son."

"You gotta listen to me, mister. We're in danger. If you don't do something, that spy will blow us all to pieces."

As they hurried me toward the gate, we passed a knot of people. The knot opened for a split second. There stood a drooling Juniper with all four paws planted on the spy he'd flattened to the ground. One of the agents let go of my arm and elbowed his way toward the commotion. The other man hustled me into a waiting car.

18

Sweet Justice

I couldn't believe it. The FBI guys jammed Wanda and Rosemarie into the back seat with me and whisked us off to their downtown office. They grilled us all afternoon, asking the same questions over and over. Mom and the Twekenberrys paced back and forth just outside the door. Finally an agent said, "We'll take it from here," and sent us home.

The next day Mom unfolded the morning paper and plopped it down on the table. She gasped and stared wide-eyed at the paper. I looked down. "Woowee!" I cried.

Triple banner headlines screamed: "GERMAN SPY CAPTURED."

My skin prickled all over. I started to read aloud, but my voice cracked and rose an octave. I had to clear my throat a couple of times before I could get reading again. "'The FBI gets their man. But this time they had the aid of local students, who alerted them to the presence of a spy at St. Johns River Shipyard. Fourteen-year-old Frank Hollahan…'"

"That's you," Mom said, beaming.

"Sure is," I said, continuing to read. "'Frank Hollahan, who lives in a sparsely populated area a few miles south of Jacksonville Beach, witnessed the spy's landing on the night of

Wednesday, December first. Frank was stargazing and, as he told this reporter, was thinking about his seafaring father when he heard the throb of a ship's motor....'"

Mom poked my arm. "Not so fast, Francis. I don't want to miss anything."

I took a breath and slowed down. "'Looking out to sea, young Frank saw the outline of a German U-boat. When asked how he knew it was a U-boat and not one of our own submarines, he replied, "Between Pops' and my identification charts, I know every ship in both the U.S. and German navies." While the submarine struggled to free itself from the sandbar, Frank saw a man come out of the sea, carrying a large chest. The man buried the chest and quickly disappeared. When young Frank looked again, the submarine was gone. Knowing he needed to alert someone, he rushed home. His mother had not yet returned from her swing shift at St. Johns River Shipyard. The Hollahans have no telephone, and their only close neighbor was out of town. Rising too late the following morning to tell his mother, a frustrated Frank brought his news to school....'"

Mom interrupted again. "You could have woken me, Francis."

"Sorry, Mom," I said and kept reading. "'Try as he might, Frank said, no one believed him. When this reporter expressed shock that his story was ignored, Frank admitted that he had a tendency to stretch the truth, a tendency he said he is trying to curb. "I guess everyone thought it was just another one of my stories," Frank said.'"

I looked at Mom, expecting some comment on that, but she waved her hand for me to continue. I did. "'Frank, with the help of classmate Rosemarie Twekenberry and beach resident Wanda Barr, gathered evidence. The truth finally prevailed at Tuesday's Bond Rally at the St. Johns River

Shipyard, where Frank boldly proclaimed a spy was present and intended harm to our citizens. Some at the rally tried to stifle Frank's outburst. Fortunately, agents of the Federal Bureau of Investigation were present. They had been alerted by the Beach Police. Captain Flagg of the Beach Police Department stated, "We had reason to believe that the boy's account was false. Nonetheless, we felt it our duty to inform the federal authorities."

"In their usual expedient manner, the FBI brought in their man, whom they captured with the aid of Wanda Barr and her feisty dog, Juniper.'"

I flipped to the next page. The entire spread was filled with details of the spy story. It said the spy admitted that he had orders to sabotage our shipyards and other key locations. The bomb planted at the train station was to destroy our morale as well as lives. The spy led the FBI to the still-buried chest. The article went on to spell out the items contained in the chest. It was unbelievable! Explosive devices disguised as pencils and lumps of coal!

After Mom heard all this, she reached over and mussed my hair. "My son, the hero. So it was the truth you told after all. Who would have guessed?"

I laughed and got the scissors from the kitchen drawer. "I'm going to send this to Pops, okay?"

"Now, won't he just be the braggingest man in the Navy?"

I walked all the way to town so I could mail the letter right away. As I passed the movie theater, Lloyd, Howard, and Joey strolled out. Seeing me, Joey began bouncing around on the soles of his feet and jabbed at my arm. "Hey, Frankie, you really saw a spy after all. Some headlines."

"Yeah, congratulations, buddy-o," Lloyd said with a big grin. "You stuck with your story like a dog with a bone. You won. Big time!"

Howard jutted his chin and gave me his thumbs-up sign. From Howard, that's high praise. I did a little strutting, accepting my well-deserved accolades. It was great getting some respect.

In January, I finally got Pops' reaction to the newspaper articles.

December 15, 1943

Dear Francis,

> *Two solid weeks without mail. You should have seen us guys scramble when word got out that mail had come aboard. When I opened the first letter, out tumbled the newspaper articles. They nearly blew off the deck, but I caught them in time. Wow! That was some news report. I'm mighty proud of you, Son.*
>
> *Between that account and the discovery that you and Mom are living in Jacksonville, you could have knocked my socks off. I had a hard time figuring the whole thing out until I finally read the letter Mom wrote about your trip down to Florida and her decision to stay. Who knows, maybe my ship will come into Mayport some day.*
>
> *Write me all the details about your spy adventure and keep those home-fires burning.*

Your Pops

And that's how Pops first heard that Mom and I had come to Jacksonville and stayed. He and Mom wrote each other every day. I wrote too, but not so often.

◂ ◂ ◂

Spring crept up on us. The beach cactus bloomed, the oak trees drizzled strips of wispy green pollen, and the guys still treated me like a hero. But when baseball season rolled around and my old exaggerations of a five hundred batting average came to nothing, they ribbed me something terrible. It's sure hard to live down a reputation.

On Sundays, whenever Mom didn't have to work, Wanda had dinner with us. I always took time to help her practice overcoming her stutter. She was getting so good at blowing to help her speak normally that she hardly had to open her lips.

June rolled around before I knew it. I was happy to see all my hard work pay off. No, that's wrong. All of Wanda's hard work paid off. She got up her courage and took her oral exams. She passed with flying colors. Boy, was she excited. All she's talked about ever since is going to college in the fall.

I took Rosemarie to our eighth-grade graduation dance. Mom made a corsage for her from our gardenia bush. "It's beautiful," Rosemarie crooned. But I told her it was nothing compared to the way she looked. Her face turned all red. Mine too. We had a swell time.

Pops wrote me lots of letters. I saved every one. It took him a long time to notice I always signed my letters "Frank." That set up a running argument by mail. Pops: "Francis is a fine name." Me: "Frank sounds more manly." Pops: "Francis was a great saint, and he was manly." Me: "I'll bet his friends called him Frank." Pops: "You win. If Frank you want to be, then Frank it is. Just don't expect your mother to ever call you anything but Francis."

On July Fourth I had such great news. I wrote that very night.

> *Dear Pops,*
>
> *Remember how Mom always told me to save my first kiss for someone really special? Well, I did! For . . . can you guess who? . . . Yep, for Rosemarie. And she kissed me right back. Woowee! What a great Fourth of July. Who needs fireworks?*
>
> *Your son, Frank*

Four days later I had to write again. It sure hurt to have to write what I did.

> *Dear Pops,*
>
> *I have some really sad news. Mr. Jolly went to Connecticut for the summer. He had gone to watch the Ringling Bros. and Barnum & Bailey Circus the afternoon the big tent caught fire. He died in the fire. Our class got together and took flowers to Mrs. Jolly. I think it cheered her up, at least a little.*
>
> *Your son, Frank*

It took me a long time to realize Mr. Jolly would never return to Jacksonville. All summer I ran on the beach trying to improve my speed, always remembering Mr. Jolly and how he cheered for me in my first football game. My running and my growing three inches helped get me on the freshman football team. I started playing quarterback and passing well, if I do say so myself. The guys still kid me when I mess up, especially Howard, but that's okay. We're all good pals.

Mom bought an old Ford clunker. As soon as she picked up her gasoline ration coupons, she took Rosemarie and me for a spin. "I hope you enjoyed that," she said. "From now on, I have to save my allotted three gallons a week for getting me back and forth to work when I have the graveyard shift."

Before I knew it, we'd been living in our chicken coop house a whole year, and Christmas was just around the corner.

Our neighbor, old man Kinchloe, hired me now and then for odd jobs. I chopped wood for his fireplace one time. He paid me fifty cents. I added that to my other savings and went Christmas shopping. I'd already bought Pops a Monopoly game. Mom mailed it with his other presents the week before Halloween. All we could do was keep our fingers crossed that they would reach him by Christmas.

At the dime store I bought Wanda a pen-and-pencil set and Rosemarie a heart-shaped locket that opens. I slipped my picture in one side. I hope she keeps it there forever. For Mom, I found one of those fancy blue bottles of Evening in Paris perfume. But the best gift I got Mom was free. I traded some of our sugar ration coupons with Mrs. Twekenberry for extra gas ration coupons for Mom. It's a good deal all around. Mrs. T. will probably give us some of the cookies she bakes with the sugar, and Mom will probably take us all for a spin.

In the middle of all our Christmas preparations, we received a mysterious letter from Pops.

Dear Edie and Frank,

Rumor has it we might be 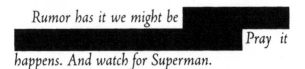 *Pray it* *happens. And watch for Superman.*

Love, Pops

I told Mom I wished I knew what I was praying for. She said, "Just pray." And I did, like I'd been doing every night since Pops left. Neither Mom nor I could figure out the Superman part.

Three days before Christmas we were in the middle of a heat wave. I knew we wouldn't see snow, but I sure hoped things would cool off. I headed for the beach, still puzzling over all those blanked out spaces in Pops' last letter.

When I came over the last rise, I saw a tall ship looming on the horizon. As soon as it began its turn to come up the coast, I realized it was an aircraft carrier. My heart flipped. Pops?

The ship turned full north, and my mouth fell open. Hundreds of sailors in their dress blues lined the rail. A huge sheet, probably a half dozen sheets sewn together, billowed over the rail and down the side of the ship. An enormous Superman was painted on the sheets. That's what Pops meant when he said watch for Superman. I'll bet every guy on the ship who had family in Jacksonville wrote home saying the same thing. That's what he asked me to pray for. That he'd make it home for shore leave.

Yahoo! I ripped off my shirt and tossed it in the air. The war wasn't over yet, but Pops was sailing toward Mayport. And that's all that mattered. I ran north along the beach, like I could catch up with the ship if I ran hard enough. But

Mayport was twelve miles away. I turned back and dashed toward home.

Pops would have his war stories to tell, and I'd have my own. He'd want all the details about the spy and how we tracked him down. He'd want to meet Rosemarie and Wanda too. And I'd introduce him to Joey and Howard and all the guys.

The sand flew off my heels as I raced down the beach. I swung past the scrub palms, turned into our path, and nearly knocked Mom off her feet.

"It's Pops!" I shouted. "His ship's headed for Mayport. He's here! In Jacksonville!

"Francis," Mom scolded, "I thought your storytelling days were over. Don't you go teasing me about a thing like that."

"I'm not teasing," I said, pulling Mom down to the water's edge. "Look!"

A strange expression crossed her face. Deep down inside she knew. I could tell. But it took her another second to believe. She started laughing and crying all at the same time. "Oh, dear heavens," she cried. "The house needs cleaning, the garden needs tending, and all we have to eat is an old chicken, tough as shoe leather." She clutched her heart. "But worse than that, I don't know if I have enough gas in the car to get us to Mayport."

"Here, Mom," I said, pulling a crumpled paper from my pocket, "an early Christmas present." Right off she recognized the gasoline ration coupons. She threw her arms around me and squealed. "What are we waiting for?" she cried.

With Mom waving the gas coupons, we hopped in the car and sped to meet Pops.

As we barreled along, Mom glanced in the rearview mirror. "Oh, Francis," she moaned, "my hair's a mess. I forgot my lipstick. And my nails are a wreck. What will Pops think?"

Mom's hair was straggly. She didn't have on a lick of makeup. And her nails were the worst I'd ever seen. But Mom's eyes shone and her face glowed. I'd never seen her look so pretty and happy. "You look swell, Mom," I said. "Absolutely swell." And that was no exaggeration.

The End

Author's Note

During World War II, 1941–1945, Nazi submarines called *Unterseebooten*, or U-boats, roamed the Atlantic Ocean attacking American and British ships at will. In June 1942, two of those U-boats put ashore eight Nazi saboteurs under cover of darkness. The spies landed on the beaches, four on Long Island, New York, and four at Ponte Vedra near Jacksonville, Florida. They brought enough money and explosives with them for a two-year campaign of terror against the American war industry and civilian population. Explosive devices, including small bombs that resembled lumps of coal and fountain pens, were found in chests buried in the sand.

Many of the details of the real spies' methods, such as secret codes, buried chests, and weapons to harm and frighten, were incorporated into the novel.

Fortunately, the real spies were quickly apprehended. They were tried, convicted, and punished for their plans to sabotage factories, take lives, and destroy the morale of the American people.

Here are some other books from Pineapple Press on related topics. For a complete catalog, visit our website at www.pineapplepress.com. Or write to Pineapple Press, P.O. Box 3889, Sarasota, Florida 34230-3889, or call (800) 746-3275.

The Treasure of Amelia Island by M.C. Finotti. Mary Kingsley, the youngest child of former slave Ana Jai Kingsley, recounts the life-changing events of December 1813. Her family lived in La Florida, a Spanish territory under siege by Patriots who see no place for freed people of color in a new Florida. Against these mighty events, Mary decides to search for a legendary pirate treasure with her brothers. This treasure hunt, filled with danger and recklessness, changes Mary forever. Ages 8–12. (hb)

Kidnapped in Key West by Edwina Raffa and Annelle Rigsby. Twelve-year-old Eddie Malone is living in the Florida Keys in 1912 when his world is turned upside down. His father, a worker on Henry Flagler's Over-Sea Railroad, is thrown into jail for stealing the railroad payroll. Eddie sets out for Key West with his faithful dog, Rex, on a daring mission to prove his father's innocence. Can he escape from the clutches of the ruthless thieves? Will he ever get back home? Will he be able to prove Pa's innocence? Ages 8–12. (hb)

Escape to the Everglades by Edwina Raffa and Annelle Rigsby. Fiction. Based on historical fact, this young adult novel tells the story of Will Cypress, a half-Seminole boy living among his mother's people during the Second Seminole War. He meets Chief Osceola and travels with him to St. Augustine. Ages 9–14. (hb)

Escape to the Everglades Teacher's Activity Guide by Edwina Raffa and Annelle Rigsby. The authors of *Escape to the Everglades* have written a teacher's manual filled with activities to help students learn more about Florida and the Seminoles. Includes references to the Sunshine State Standards.

Blood Moon Rider by Zack C. Waters. When his Marine father is killed in WWII, young Harley Wallace is exiled to the Florida cattle ranch of his bitter, badly scarred grandfather. The murder of a cowman and the disappearance of Grandfather Wallace leads Harley and his new friend Beth on a wild ride through the swamps and into the midst of a conspiracy of evil. Ages 9–14. (hb)

Solomon by Marilyn Bishop Shaw. Young Solomon Freeman and his parents, Moses and Lela, survive the Civil War, gain their freedom, and gamble their dreams, risking their very existence on a homestead in the remote environs of north central Florida. Ages 9–14. (hb)

A Land Remembered: Student Edition by Patrick D. Smith. This well-loved, best-selling novel tells the story of three generations of the MacIveys, a Florida family battling the hardships of the frontier, and how they rise from a dirt-poor cracker life to the wealth and standing of real estate tycoons. Now available to young readers in two volumes. Ages 9 and up. (hb & pb)

Hunted Like a Wolf: The Story of the Seminole War by Milton Meltzer. Offers a look at the events, players, and political motives leading to the Seminole War and the near extermination of a people. Ages 12 and up. (hb)

CPSIA information can be obtained
at www.ICGtesting.com
Printed in the USA
BVHW03s2019180718
521861BV00005BA/16/P

9 781561 642458